NO LONGER PROPERTY OF
SEATTLE PUBLIC LIBRARY

D0446353

DISNEP

A
CHRISTMAS
CAROL

STARRING

SCROOGE McDUCK

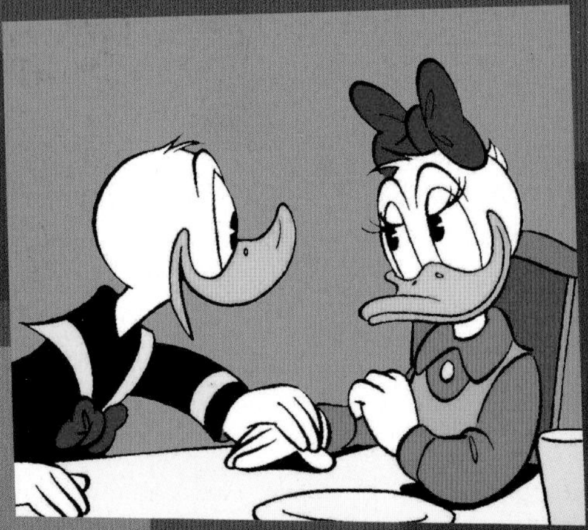

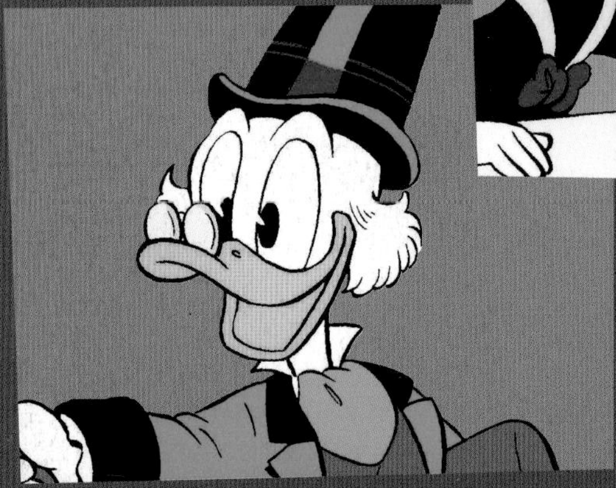

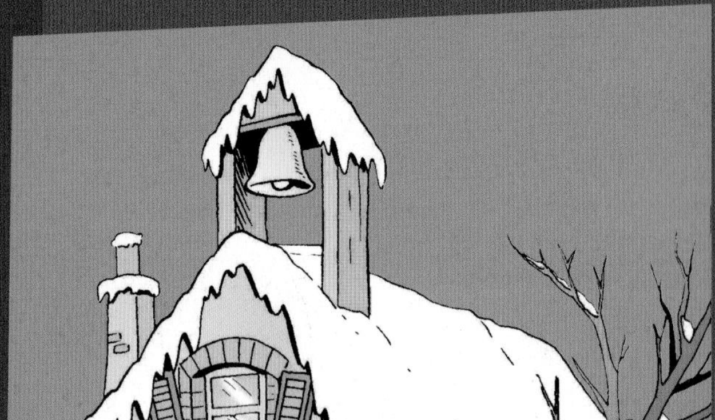

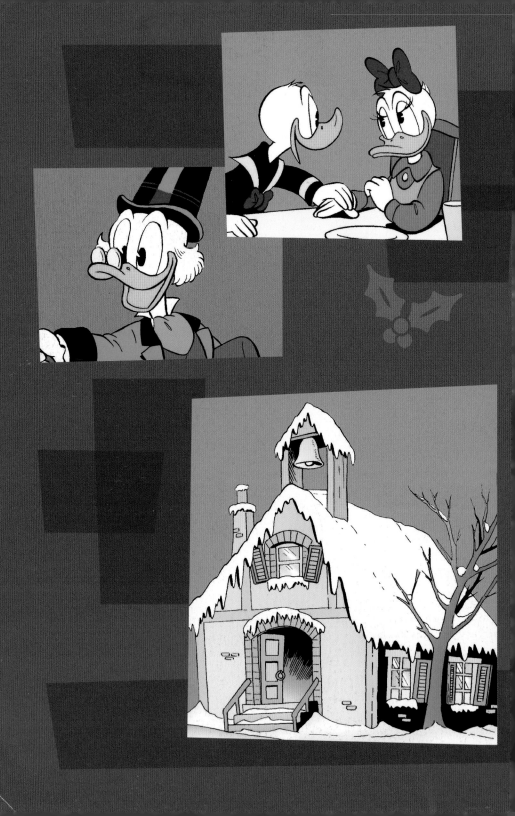

DISNEY

A CHRISTMAS CAROL

STARRING
SCROOGE McDUCK

Script by .... **GUIDO MARTINA**

Art by ....**JOSÉ COLOMER FONTS**

Based on the classic novella by
CHARLES DICKENS

DARK HORSE BOOKS

DARK HORSE BOOKS

President and Publisher . . . . MIKE RICHARDSON

Collection Editor . . . . FREDDYE MILLER

Collection Assistant Editor . . . . JUDY KHUU

Designer . . . . SKYLER WEISSENFLUH

Digital Art Technician . . . . SAMANTHA HUMMER

NEIL HANKERSON Executive Vice President • TOM WEDDLE Chief Financial Officer • RANDY STRADLEY Vice President of Publishing • NICK McWHORTER Chief Business Development Officer • DALE LaFOUNTAIN Chief Information Officer • MATT PARKINSON Vice President of Marketing • CARA NIECE Vice President of Production and Scheduling • MARK BERNARDI Vice President of Book Trade and Digital Sales • KEN LIZZI General Counsel • DAVE MARSHALL Editor in Chief • DAVEY ESTRADA Editorial Director • CHRIS WARNER Senior Books Editor • CARY GRAZZINI Director of Specialty Projects • LIA RIBACCHI Art Director • VANESSA TODD-HOLMES Director of Print Purchasing • MATT DRYER Director of Digital Art and Prepress • MICHAEL GOMBOS Senior Director of Licensed Publications • KARI YADRO Director of Custom Programs • KARI TORSON Director of International Licensing • SEAN BRICE Director of Trade Sales

DISNEY PUBLISHING WORLDWIDE GLOBAL MAGAZINES, COMICS AND PARTWORKS

PUBLISHER Lynn Waggoner • EDITORIAL TEAM Bianca Coletti (Director, Magazines), Guido Frazzini (Director, Comics), Carlotta Quattrocolo (Executive Editor), Stefano Ambrosio (Executive Editor, New IP), Camilla Vedove (Senior Manager, Editorial Development), Behnoosh Khalili (Senior Editor), Julie Dorris (Senior Editor), Mina Riazi (Assistant Editor) • DESIGN Enrico Soave (Senior Designer) • ART Ken Shue (VP, Global Art), Manny Mederos (Senior Illustration Manager, Comics and Magazines), Roberto Santillo (Creative Director), Marco Ghiglione (Creative Manager), Stefano Attardi (Illustration Manager) • PORTFOLIO MANAGEMENT Olivia Ciancarelli (Director) • BUSINESS & MARKETING Mariantonietta Galla (Senior Manager, Franchise), Virpi Korhonen (Editorial Manager)

Published by Dark Horse Books
A division of Dark Horse Comics LLC
10956 SE Main Street
Milwaukie, OR 97222

DarkHorse.com
To find a comics shop in your area,
visit comicshoplocator.com

First edition: September 2019
ISBN 978-1-50671-215-4
Digital 978-1-50671-210-9

1 3 5 7 9 10 8 6 4 2
Printed in China

DISNEY A CHRISTMAS CAROL, STARRING SCROOGE McDUCK

Disney A Christmas Carol Copyright © 2019 Disney Enterprises, Inc. All Rights Reserved. Dark Horse Books® and the Dark Horse logo are registered trademarks of Dark Horse Comics LLC. All rights reserved. No portion of this publication may be reproduced or transmitted, in any form or by any means, without the express written permission of Dark Horse Comics LLC. Names, characters, places, and incidents featured in this publication either are the product of the author's imagination or are used fictitiously. Any resemblance to actual persons (living or dead), events, institutions, or locales, without satiric intent, is coincidental.

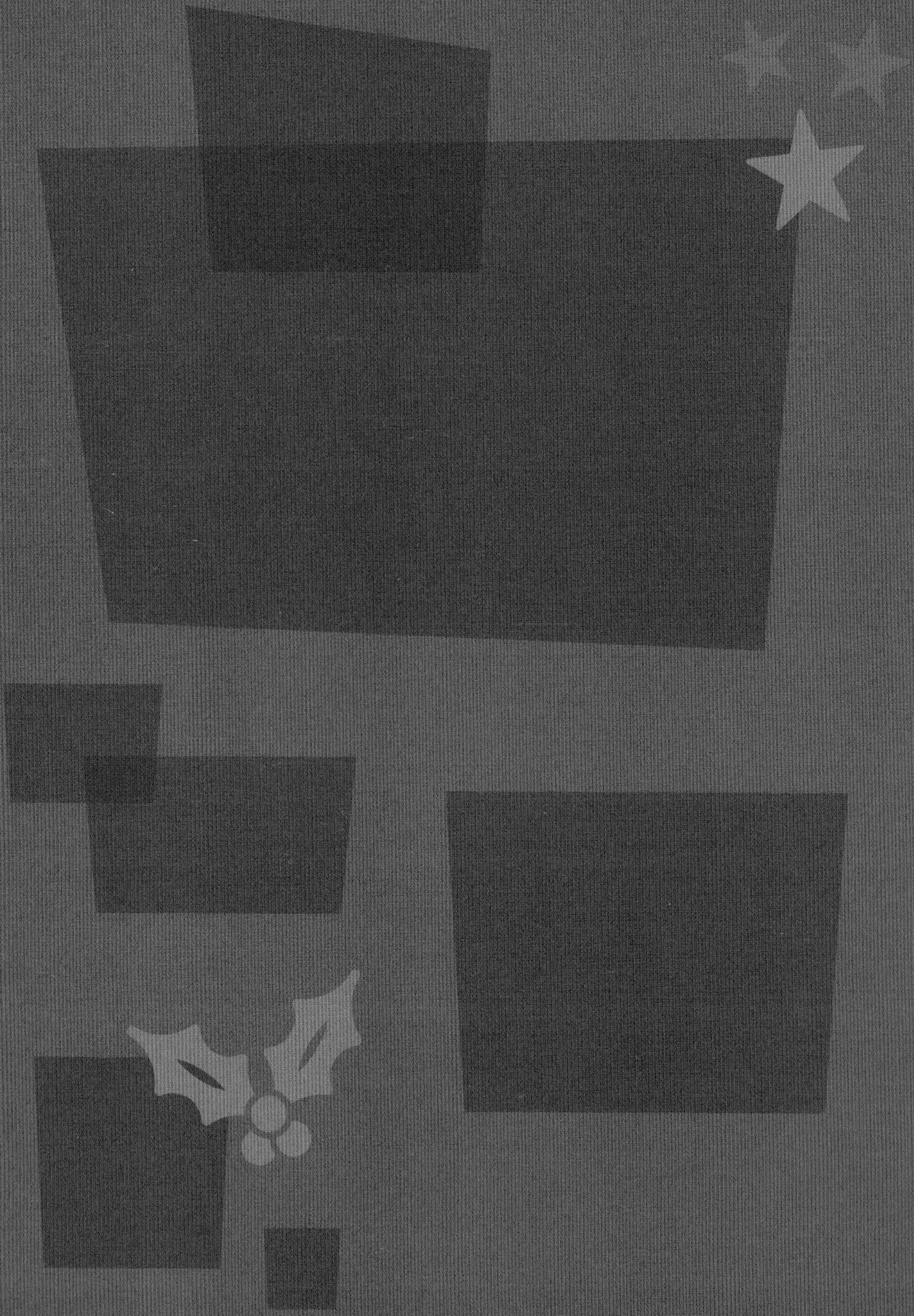

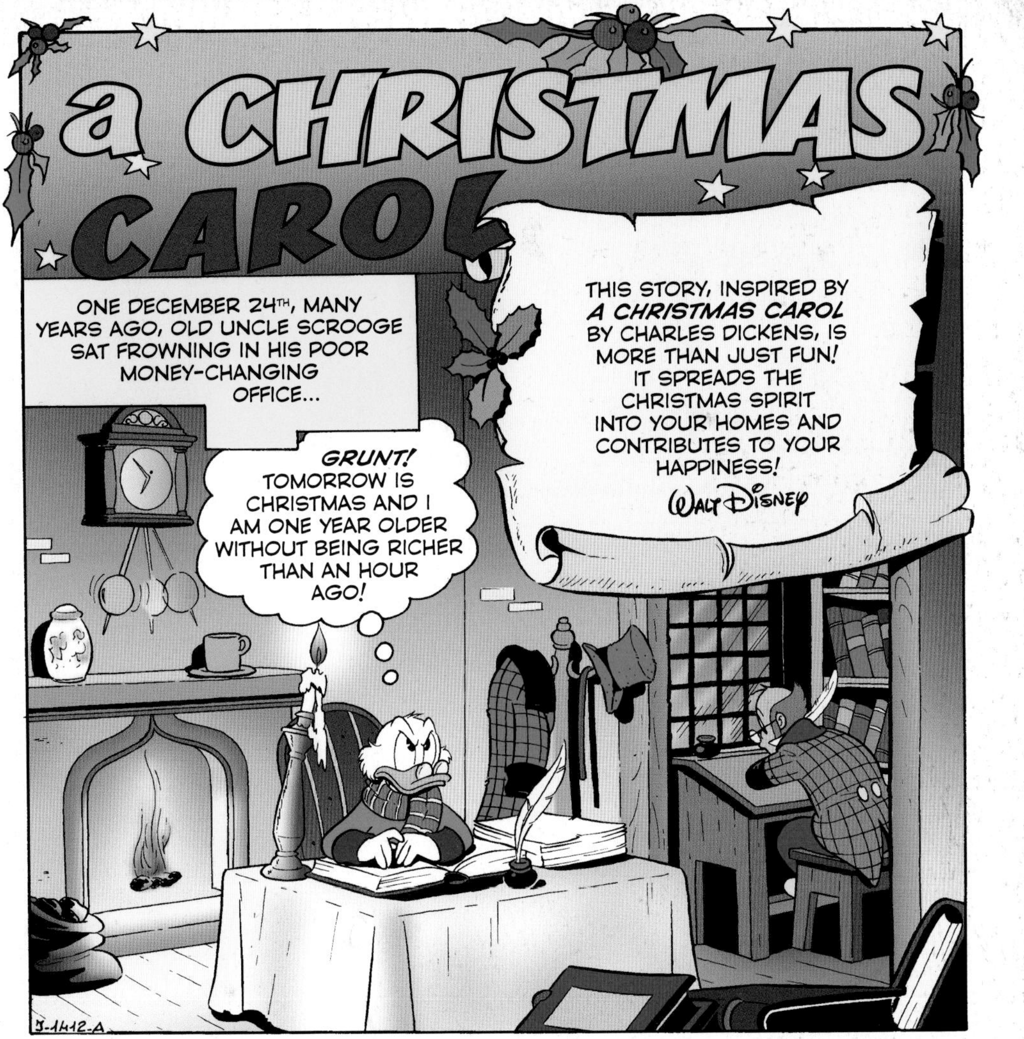
a CHRISTMAS CAROL
ONE DECEMBER 24TH, MANY YEARS AGO, OLD UNCLE SCROOGE SAT FROWNING IN HIS POOR MONEY-CHANGING OFFICE...
THIS STORY, INSPIRED BY *A CHRISTMAS CAROL* BY CHARLES DICKENS, IS MORE THAN JUST FUN! IT SPREADS THE CHRISTMAS SPIRIT INTO YOUR HOMES AND CONTRIBUTES TO YOUR HAPPINESS!
WALT DISNEY
GRUNT! TOMORROW IS CHRISTMAS AND I AM ONE YEAR OLDER WITHOUT BEING RICHER THAN AN HOUR AGO!
J-1412-A

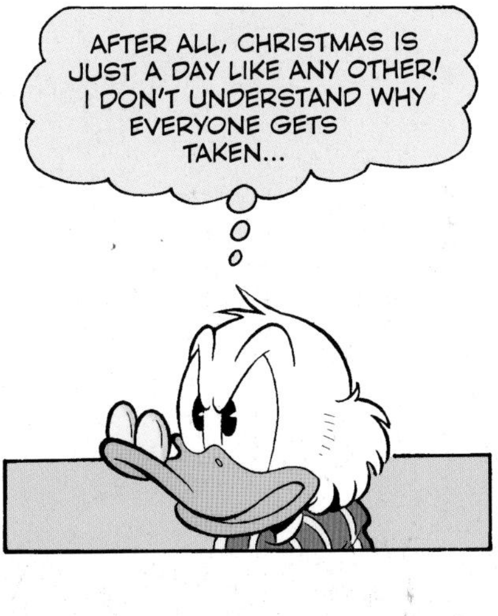
AFTER ALL, CHRISTMAS IS JUST A DAY LIKE ANY OTHER! I DON'T UNDERSTAND WHY EVERYONE GETS TAKEN...

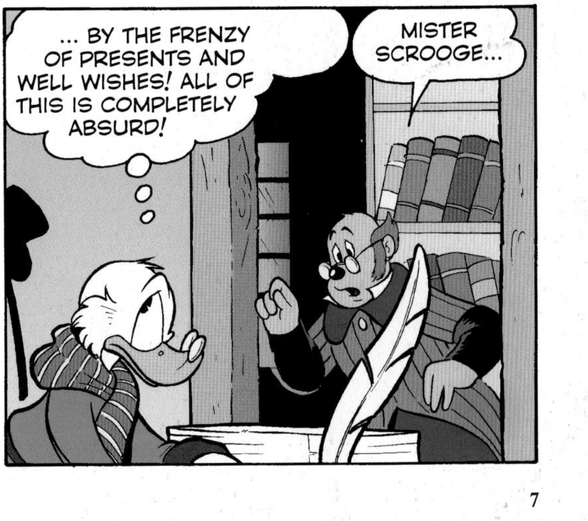
... BY THE FRENZY OF PRESENTS AND WELL WISHES! ALL OF THIS IS COMPLETELY ABSURD!
MISTER SCROOGE...

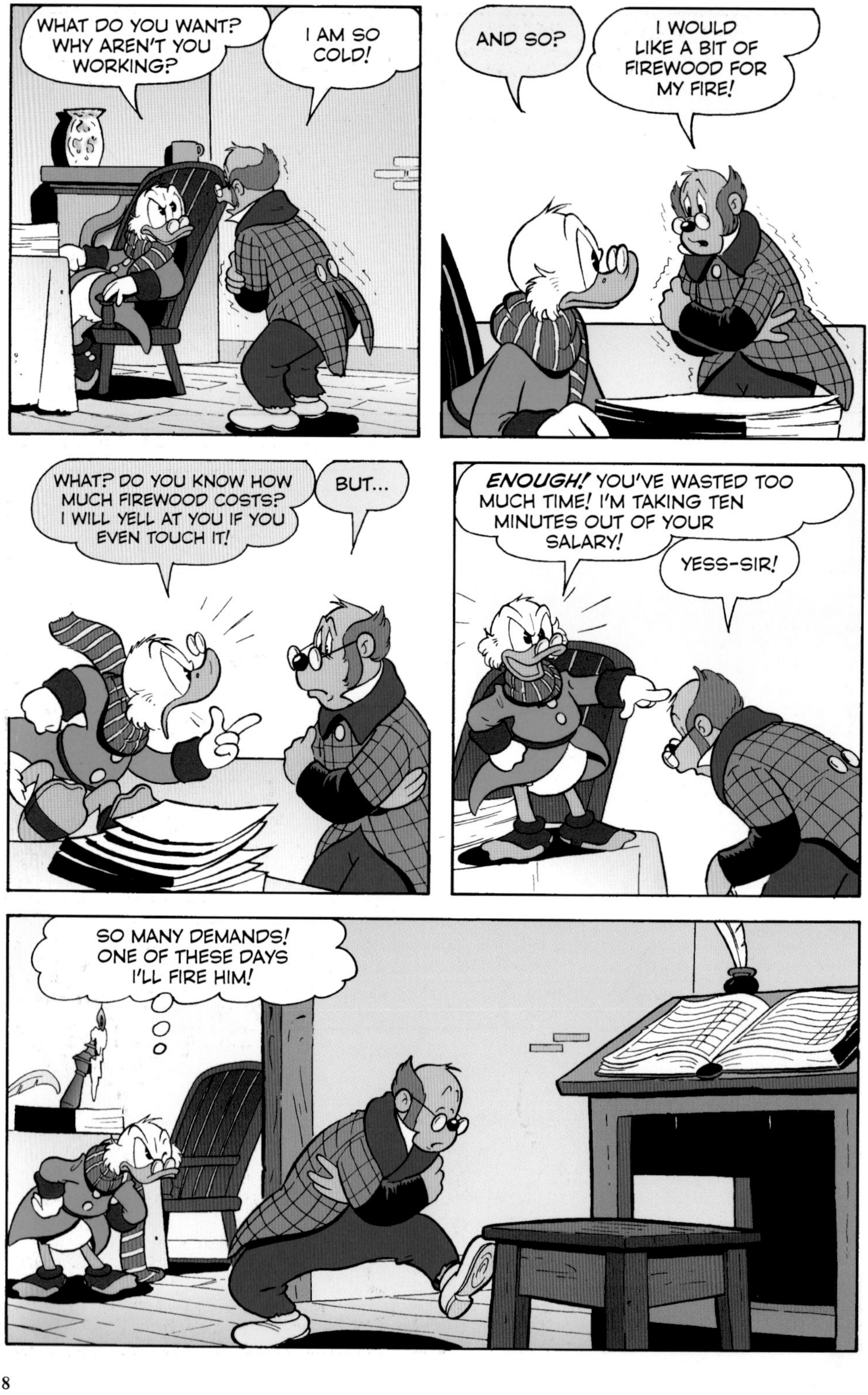
WHAT DO YOU WANT? WHY AREN'T YOU WORKING?
I AM SO COLD!
AND SO?
I WOULD LIKE A BIT OF FIREWOOD FOR MY FIRE!
WHAT? DO YOU KNOW HOW MUCH FIREWOOD COSTS? I WILL YELL AT YOU IF YOU EVEN TOUCH IT!
BUT...
ENOUGH! YOU'VE WASTED TOO MUCH TIME! I'M TAKING TEN MINUTES OUT OF YOUR SALARY!
YESS-SIR!
SO MANY DEMANDS! ONE OF THESE DAYS I'LL FIRE HIM!

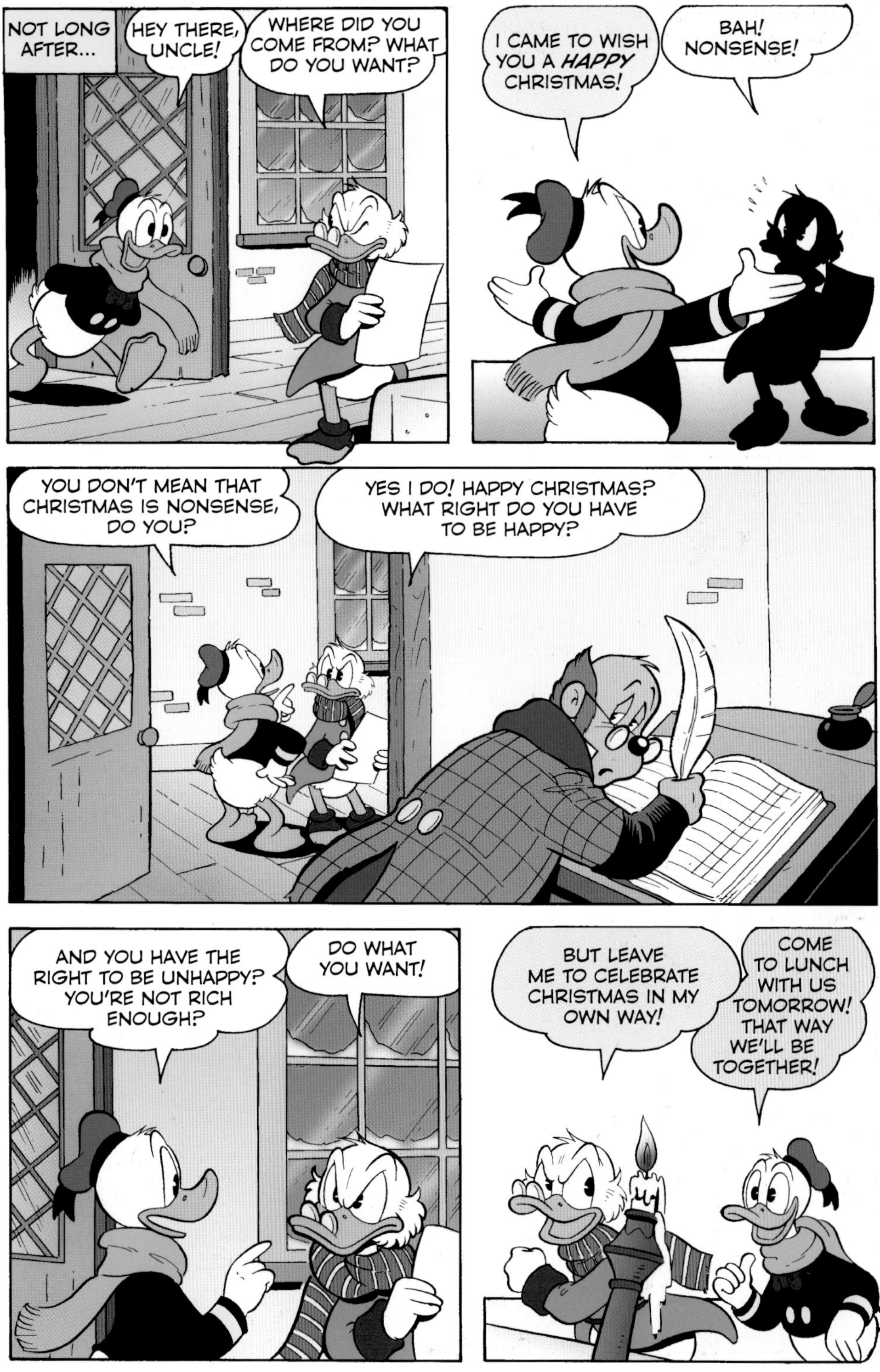
NOT LONG AFTER...
HEY THERE, UNCLE!
WHERE DID YOU COME FROM? WHAT DO YOU WANT?
I CAME TO WISH YOU A *HAPPY* CHRISTMAS!
BAH! NONSENSE!
YOU DON'T MEAN THAT CHRISTMAS IS NONSENSE, DO YOU?
YES I *DO*! HAPPY CHRISTMAS? WHAT RIGHT DO YOU HAVE TO BE HAPPY?
AND YOU HAVE THE RIGHT TO BE UNHAPPY? YOU'RE NOT RICH ENOUGH?
DO WHAT YOU WANT!
BUT LEAVE ME TO CELEBRATE CHRISTMAS IN MY OWN WAY!
COME TO LUNCH WITH US TOMORROW! THAT WAY WE'LL BE TOGETHER!

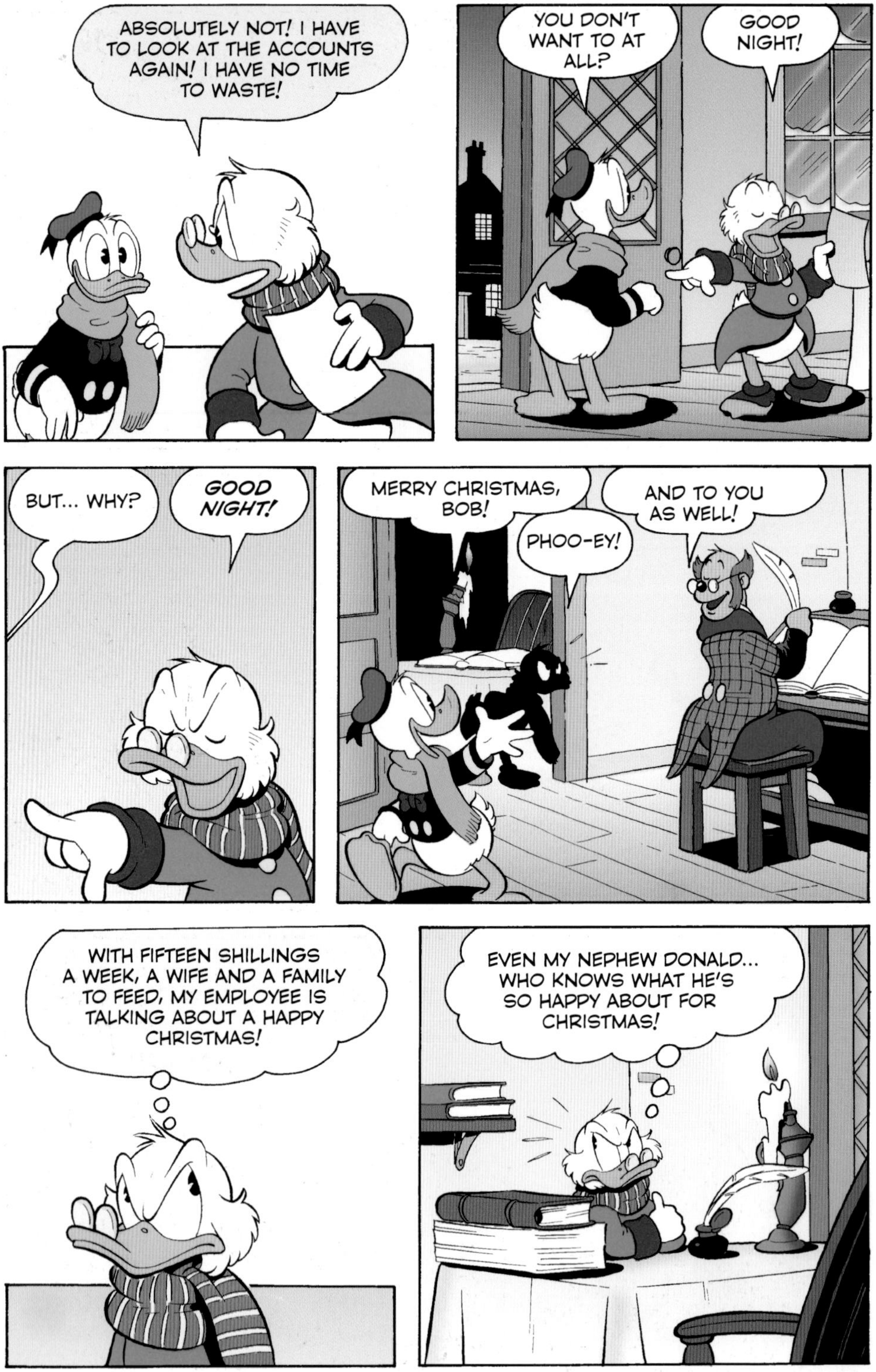
ABSOLUTELY NOT! I HAVE TO LOOK AT THE ACCOUNTS AGAIN! I HAVE NO TIME TO WASTE!
YOU DON'T WANT TO AT ALL?
GOOD NIGHT!
BUT... WHY?
GOOD NIGHT!
MERRY CHRISTMAS, BOB!
PHOO-EY!
AND TO YOU AS WELL!
WITH FIFTEEN SHILLINGS A WEEK, A WIFE AND A FAMILY TO FEED, MY EMPLOYEE IS TALKING ABOUT A HAPPY CHRISTMAS!
EVEN MY NEPHEW DONALD... WHO KNOWS WHAT HE'S SO HAPPY ABOUT FOR CHRISTMAS!

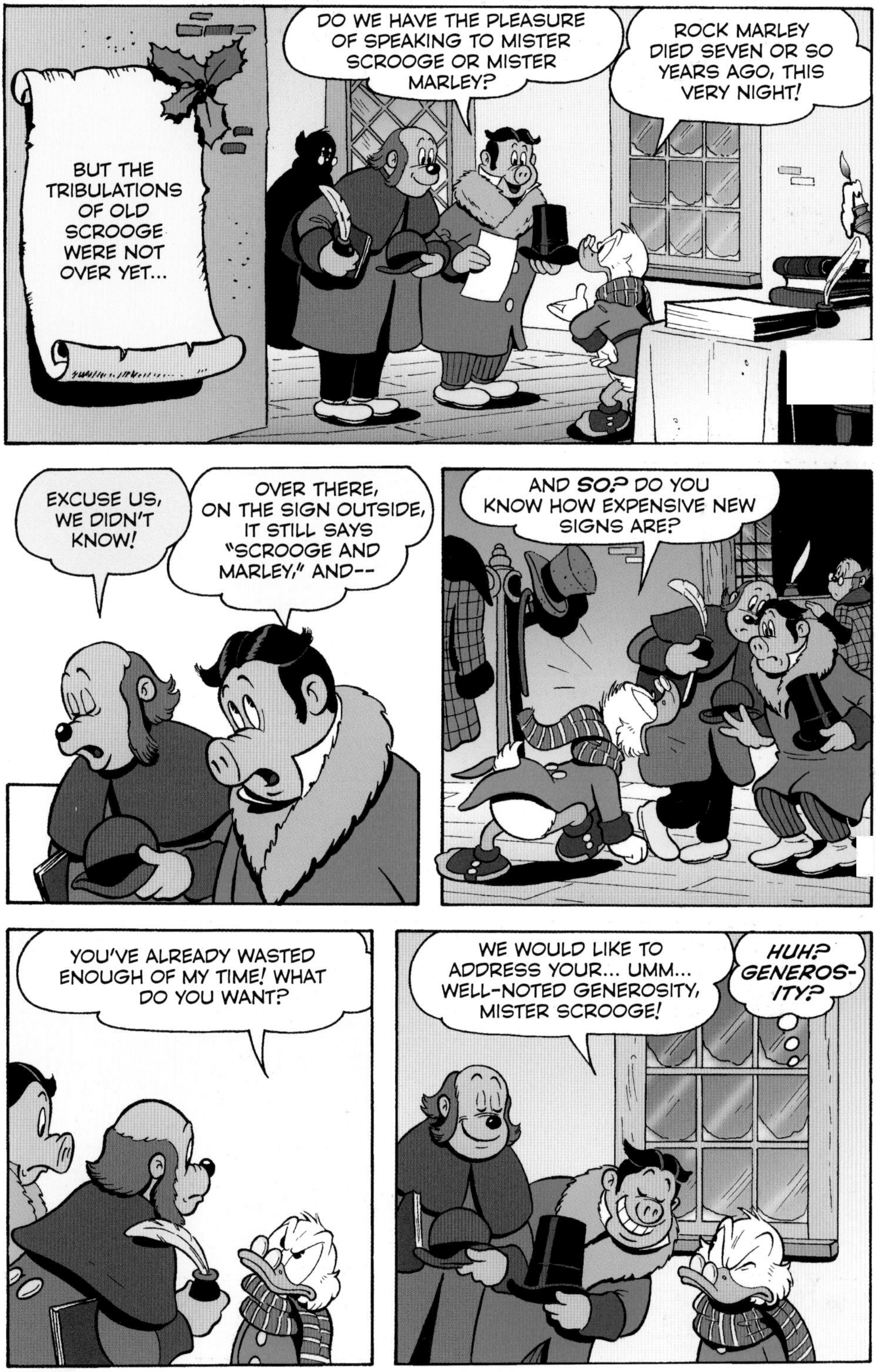

BUT THE TRIBULATIONS OF OLD SCROOGE WERE NOT OVER YET...
DO WE HAVE THE PLEASURE OF SPEAKING TO MISTER SCROOGE OR MISTER MARLEY?
ROCK MARLEY DIED SEVEN OR SO YEARS AGO, THIS VERY NIGHT!
EXCUSE US, WE DIDN'T KNOW!
OVER THERE, ON THE SIGN OUTSIDE, IT STILL SAYS "SCROOGE AND MARLEY," AND--
AND SO? DO YOU KNOW HOW EXPENSIVE NEW SIGNS ARE?
YOU'VE ALREADY WASTED ENOUGH OF MY TIME! WHAT DO YOU WANT?
WE WOULD LIKE TO ADDRESS YOUR... UMM... WELL-NOTED GENEROSITY, MISTER SCROOGE!
HUH? GENEROS-ITY?

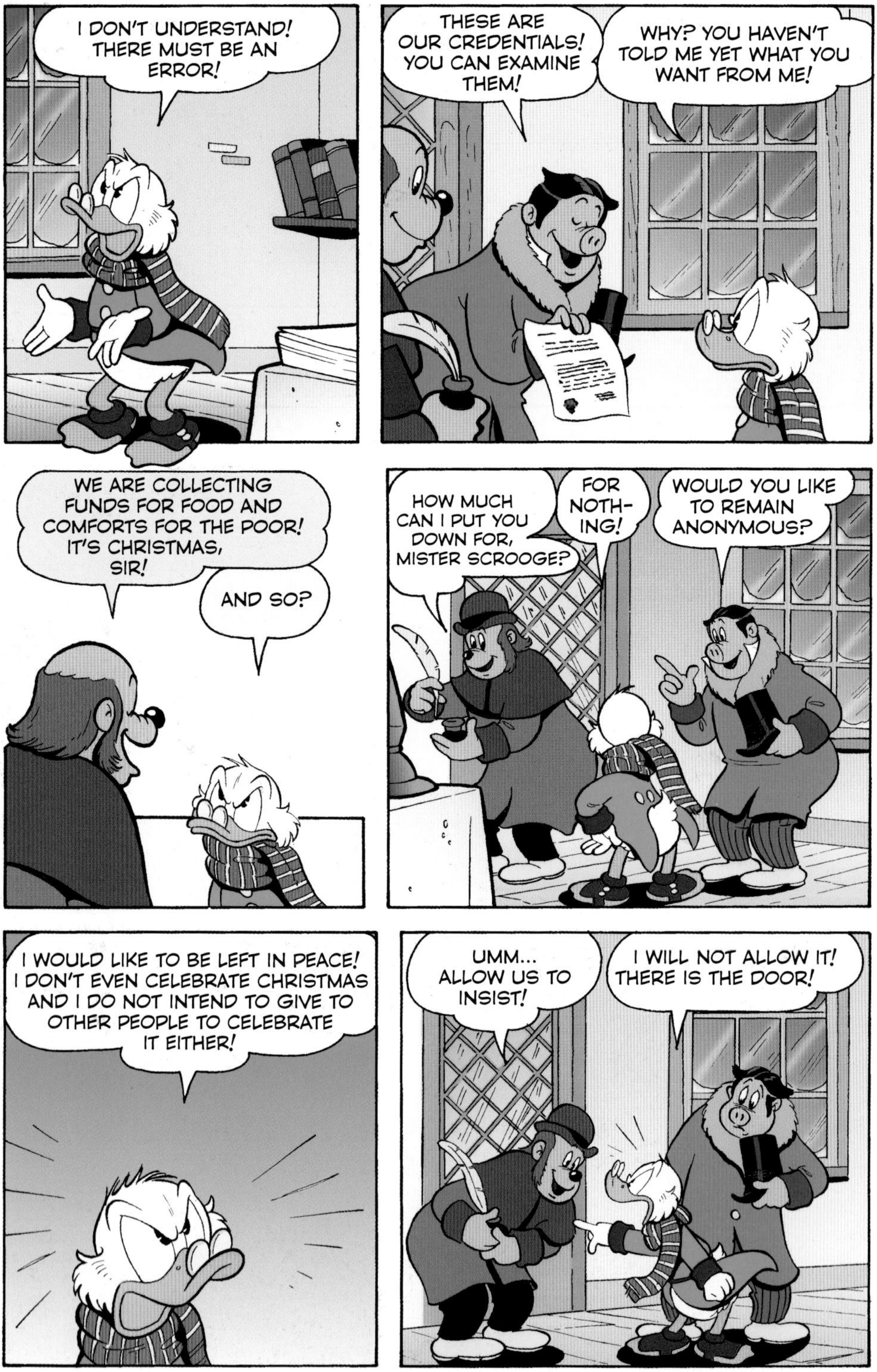
I DON'T UNDERSTAND! THERE MUST BE AN ERROR!
THESE ARE OUR CREDENTIALS! YOU CAN EXAMINE THEM!
WHY? YOU HAVEN'T TOLD ME YET WHAT YOU WANT FROM ME!
WE ARE COLLECTING FUNDS FOR FOOD AND COMFORTS FOR THE POOR! IT'S CHRISTMAS, SIR!
AND SO?
HOW MUCH CAN I PUT YOU DOWN FOR, MISTER SCROOGE?
FOR NOTH-ING!
WOULD YOU LIKE TO REMAIN ANONYMOUS?
I WOULD LIKE TO BE LEFT IN PEACE! I DON'T EVEN CELEBRATE CHRISTMAS AND I DO NOT INTEND TO GIVE TO OTHER PEOPLE TO CELEBRATE IT EITHER!
UMM... ALLOW US TO INSIST!
I WILL NOT ALLOW IT! THERE IS THE DOOR!

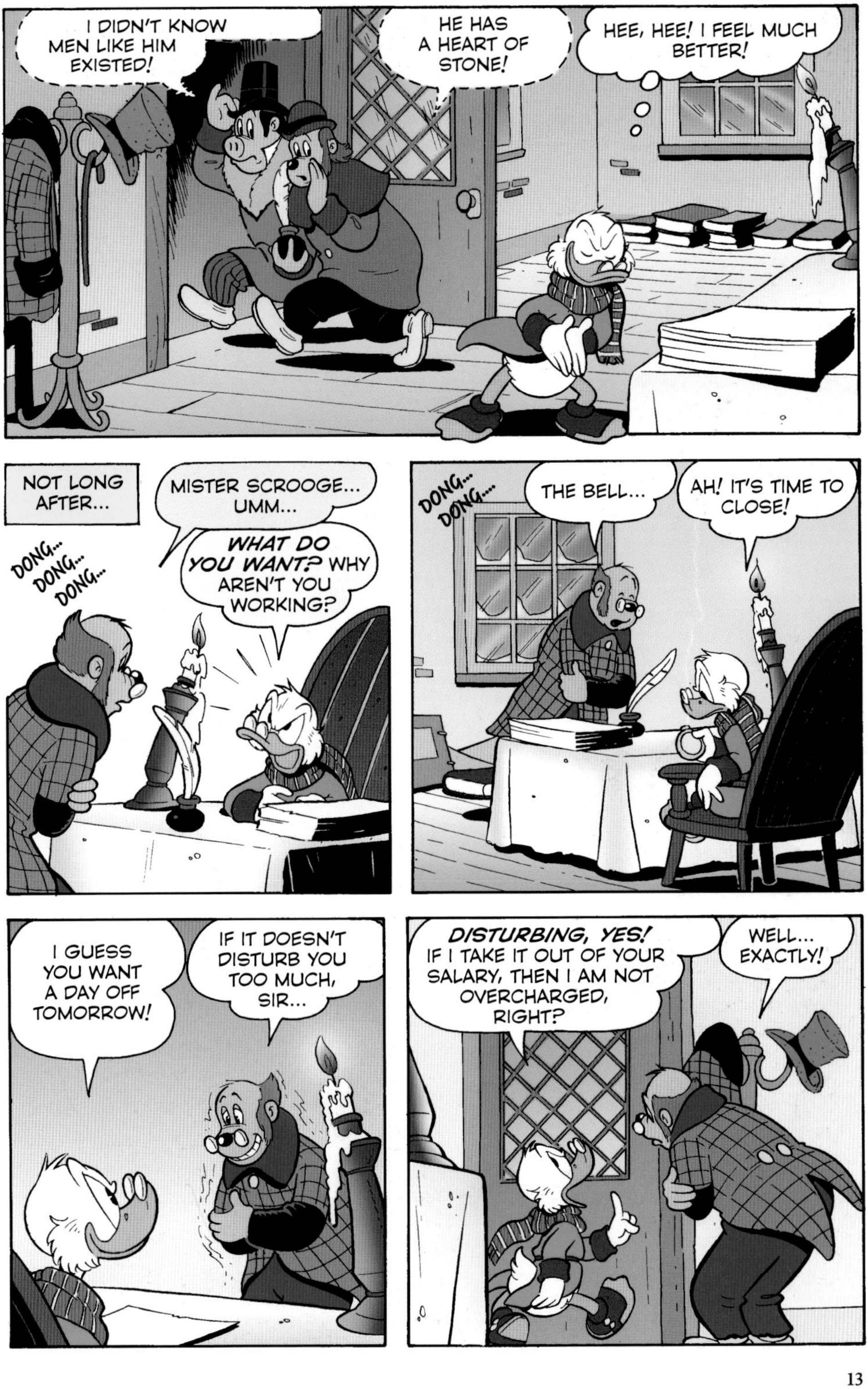
I DIDN'T KNOW MEN LIKE HIM EXISTED!
HE HAS A HEART OF STONE!
HEE, HEE! I FEEL MUCH BETTER!
NOT LONG AFTER...
MISTER SCROOGE... UMM...
DONG... DONG... DONG...
WHAT DO YOU WANT? WHY AREN'T YOU WORKING?
DONG... DONG...
THE BELL...
AH! IT'S TIME TO CLOSE!
I GUESS YOU WANT A DAY OFF TOMORROW!
IF IT DOESN'T DISTURB YOU TOO MUCH, SIR...
DISTURBING, YES! IF I TAKE IT OUT OF YOUR SALARY, THEN I AM NOT OVERCHARGED, RIGHT?
WELL... EXACTLY!

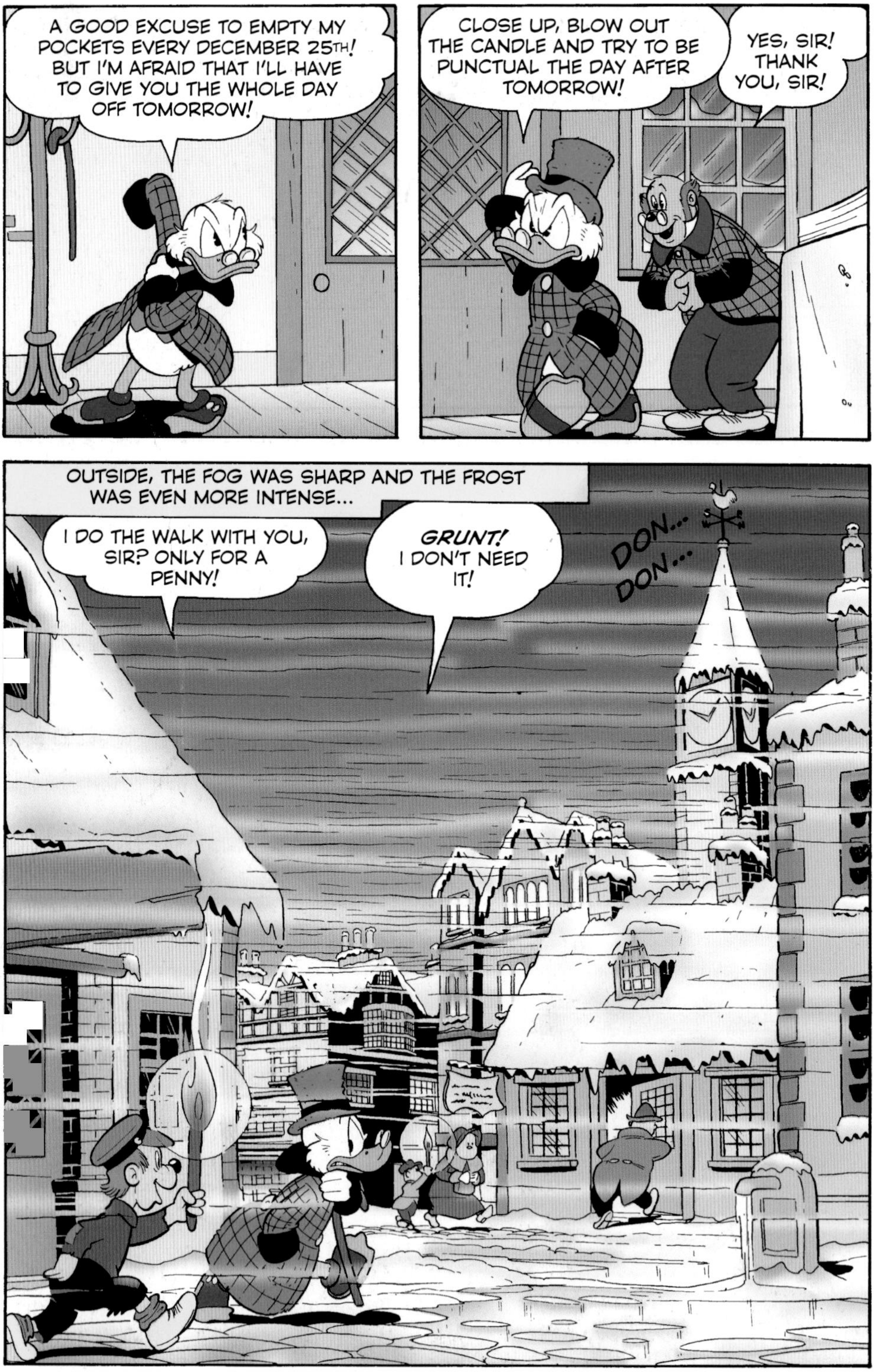
A GOOD EXCUSE TO EMPTY MY POCKETS EVERY DECEMBER 25TH! BUT I'M AFRAID THAT I'LL HAVE TO GIVE YOU THE WHOLE DAY OFF TOMORROW!
CLOSE UP, BLOW OUT THE CANDLE AND TRY TO BE PUNCTUAL THE DAY AFTER TOMORROW!
YES, SIR! THANK YOU, SIR!
OUTSIDE, THE FOG WAS SHARP AND THE FROST WAS EVEN MORE INTENSE...
I DO THE WALK WITH YOU, SIR? ONLY FOR A PENNY!
GRUNT! I DON'T NEED IT!
DON... DON...

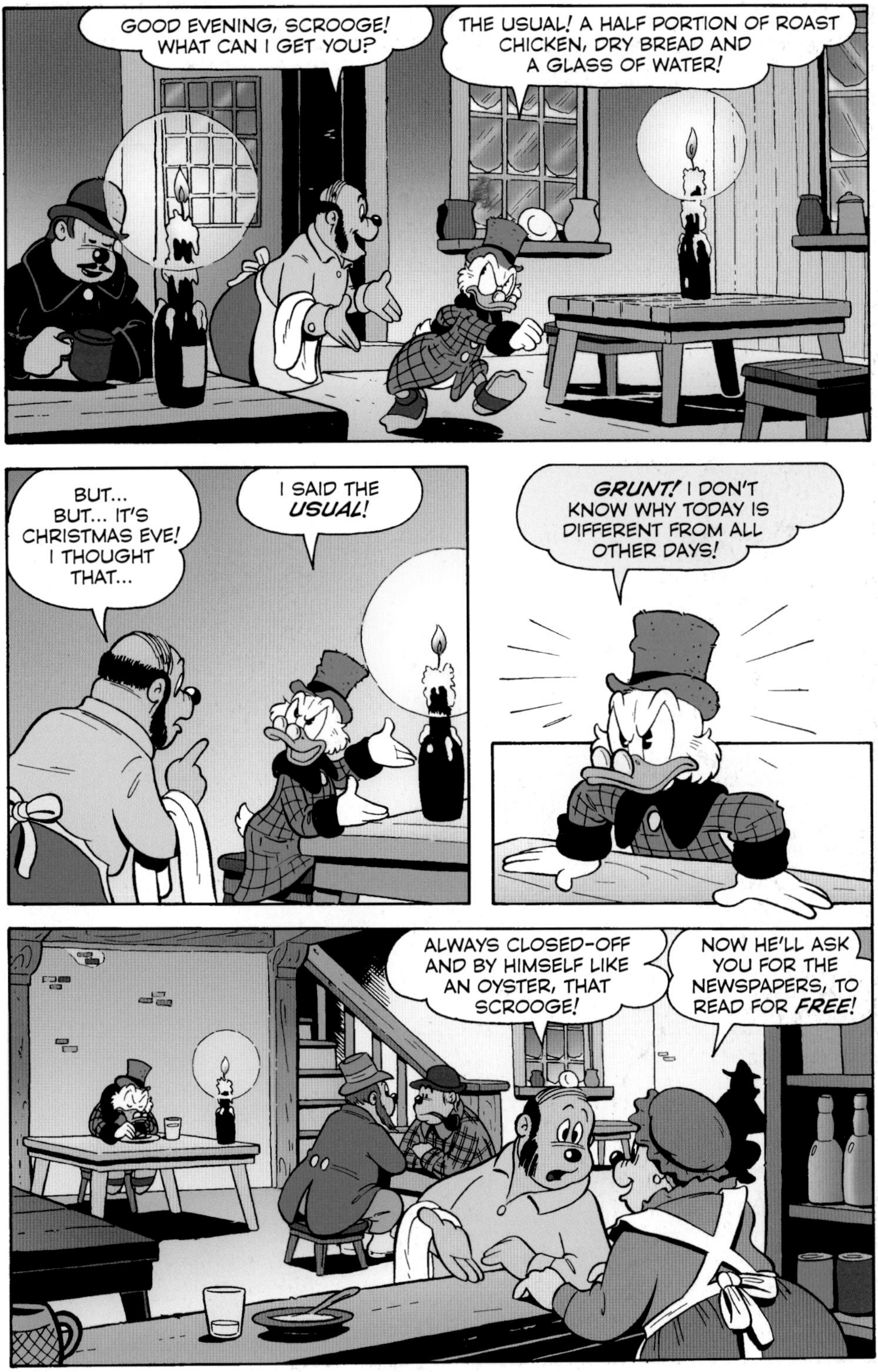
GOOD EVENING, SCROOGE! WHAT CAN I GET YOU?
THE USUAL! A HALF PORTION OF ROAST CHICKEN, DRY BREAD AND A GLASS OF WATER!
BUT... BUT... IT'S CHRISTMAS EVE! I THOUGHT THAT...
I SAID THE *USUAL*!
GRUNT! I DON'T KNOW WHY TODAY IS DIFFERENT FROM ALL OTHER DAYS!
ALWAYS CLOSED-OFF AND BY HIMSELF LIKE AN OYSTER, THAT SCROOGE!
NOW HE'LL ASK YOU FOR THE NEWSPAPERS, TO READ FOR *FREE*!

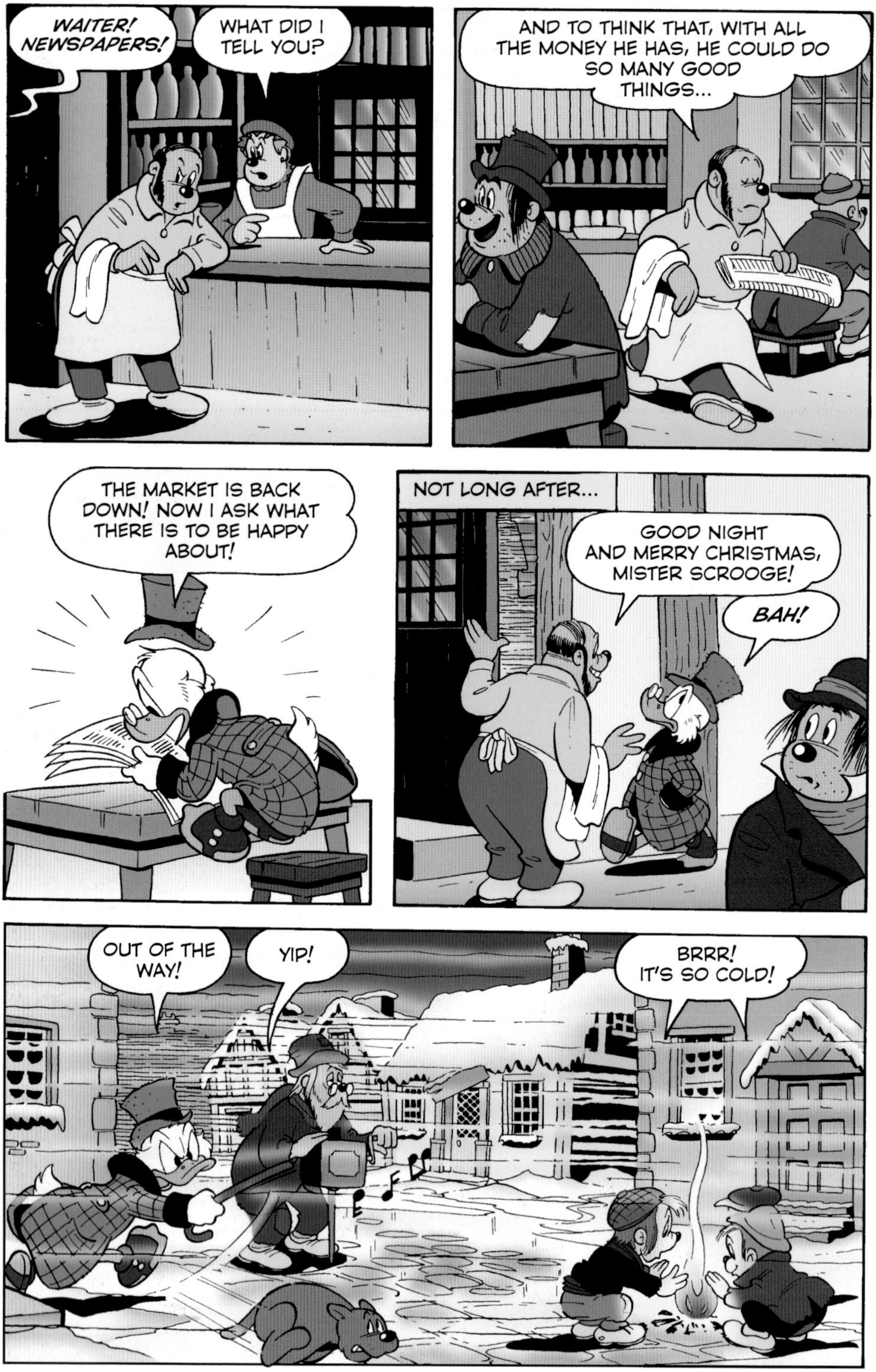
WAITER! NEWSPAPERS!
WHAT DID I TELL YOU?
AND TO THINK THAT, WITH ALL THE MONEY HE HAS, HE COULD DO SO MANY GOOD THINGS...
THE MARKET IS BACK DOWN! NOW I ASK WHAT THERE IS TO BE HAPPY ABOUT!
NOT LONG AFTER...
GOOD NIGHT AND MERRY CHRISTMAS, MISTER SCROOGE!
BAH!
OUT OF THE WAY!
YIP!
BRRR! IT'S SO COLD!

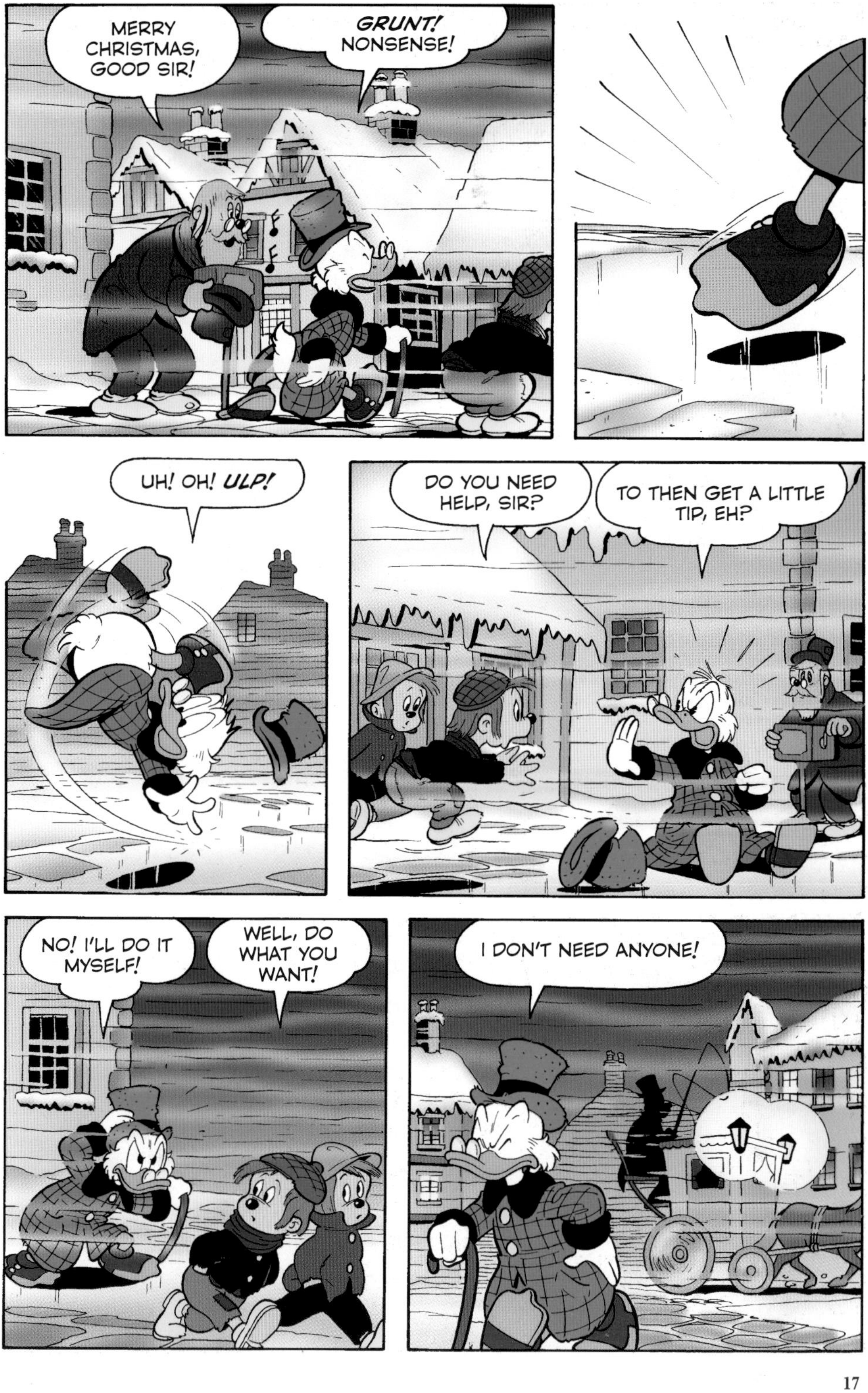
MERRY CHRISTMAS, GOOD SIR!
GRUNT! NONSENSE!
UH! OH! ULP!
DO YOU NEED HELP, SIR?
TO THEN GET A LITTLE TIP, EH?
NO! I'LL DO IT MYSELF!
WELL, DO WHAT YOU WANT!
I DON'T NEED ANYONE!

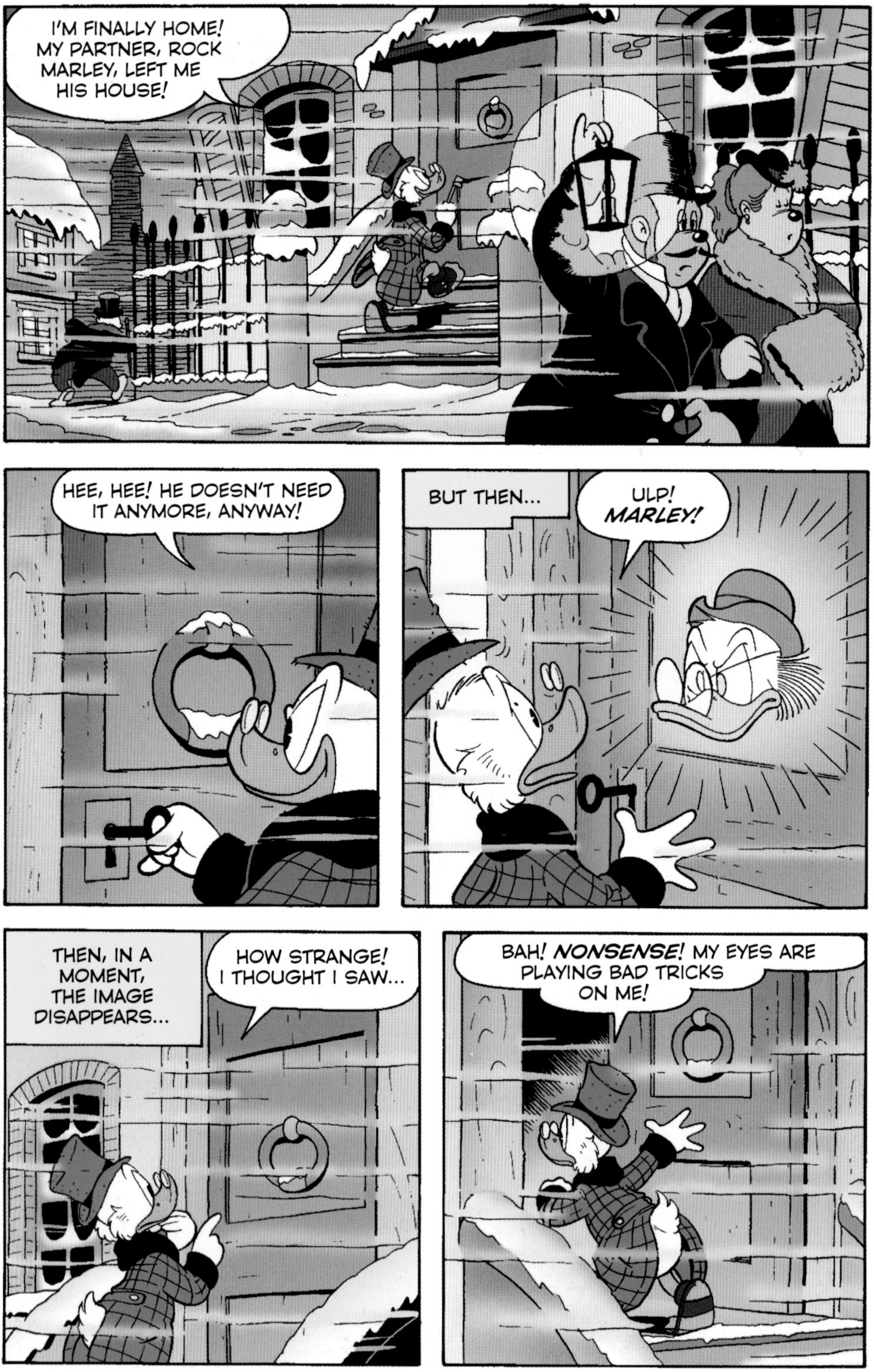

I'M FINALLY HOME! MY PARTNER, ROCK MARLEY, LEFT ME HIS HOUSE!
HEE, HEE! HE DOESN'T NEED IT ANYMORE, ANYWAY!
BUT THEN...
ULP! MARLEY!
THEN, IN A MOMENT, THE IMAGE DISAPPEARS...
HOW STRANGE! I THOUGHT I SAW...
BAH! NONSENSE! MY EYES ARE PLAYING BAD TRICKS ON ME!

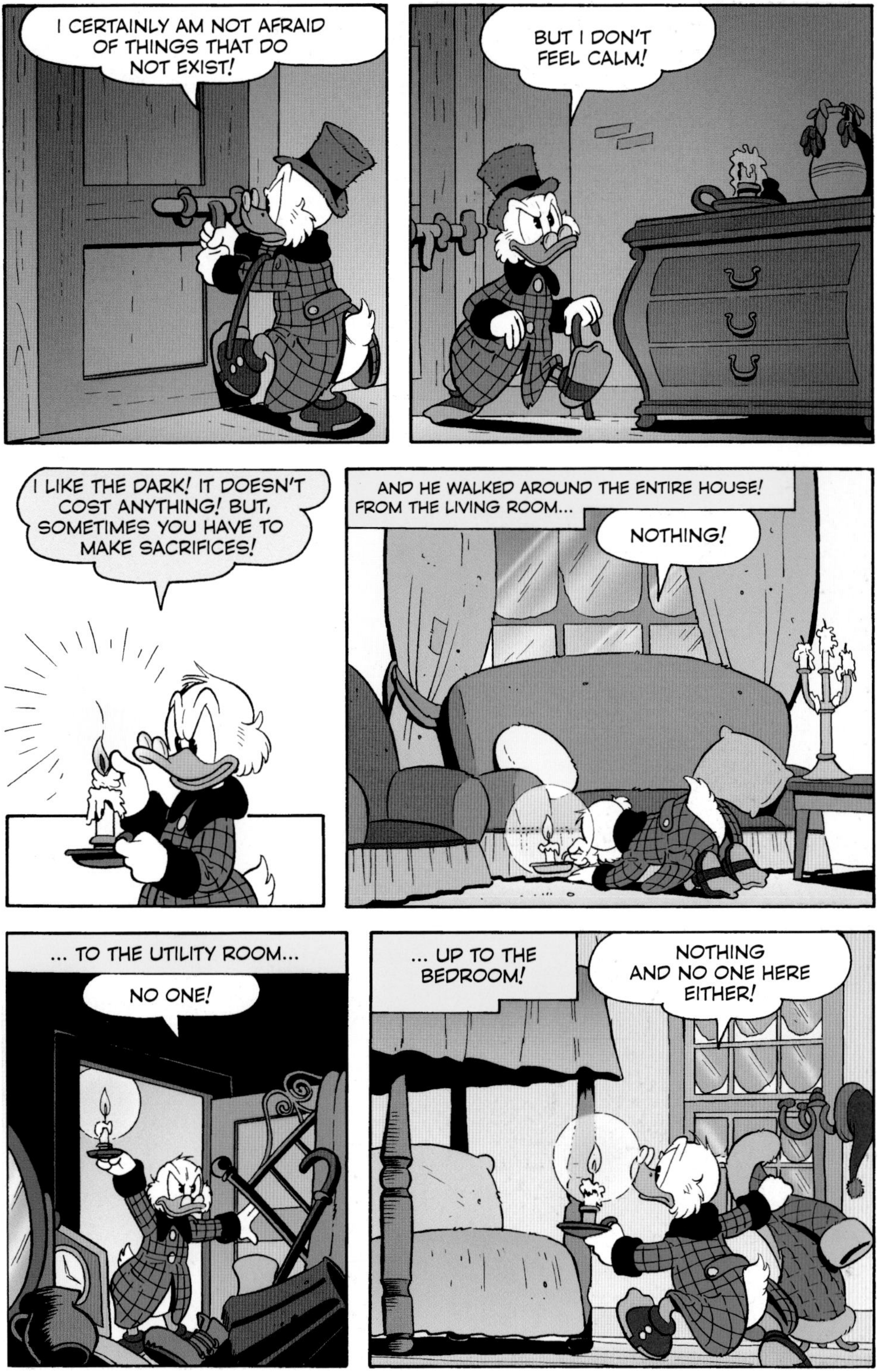

I CERTAINLY AM NOT AFRAID OF THINGS THAT DO NOT EXIST!
BUT I DON'T FEEL CALM!
I LIKE THE DARK! IT DOESN'T COST ANYTHING! BUT, SOMETIMES YOU HAVE TO MAKE SACRIFICES!
AND HE WALKED AROUND THE ENTIRE HOUSE! FROM THE LIVING ROOM...
NOTHING!
... TO THE UTILITY ROOM...
NO ONE!
... UP TO THE BEDROOM!
NOTHING AND NO ONE HERE EITHER!

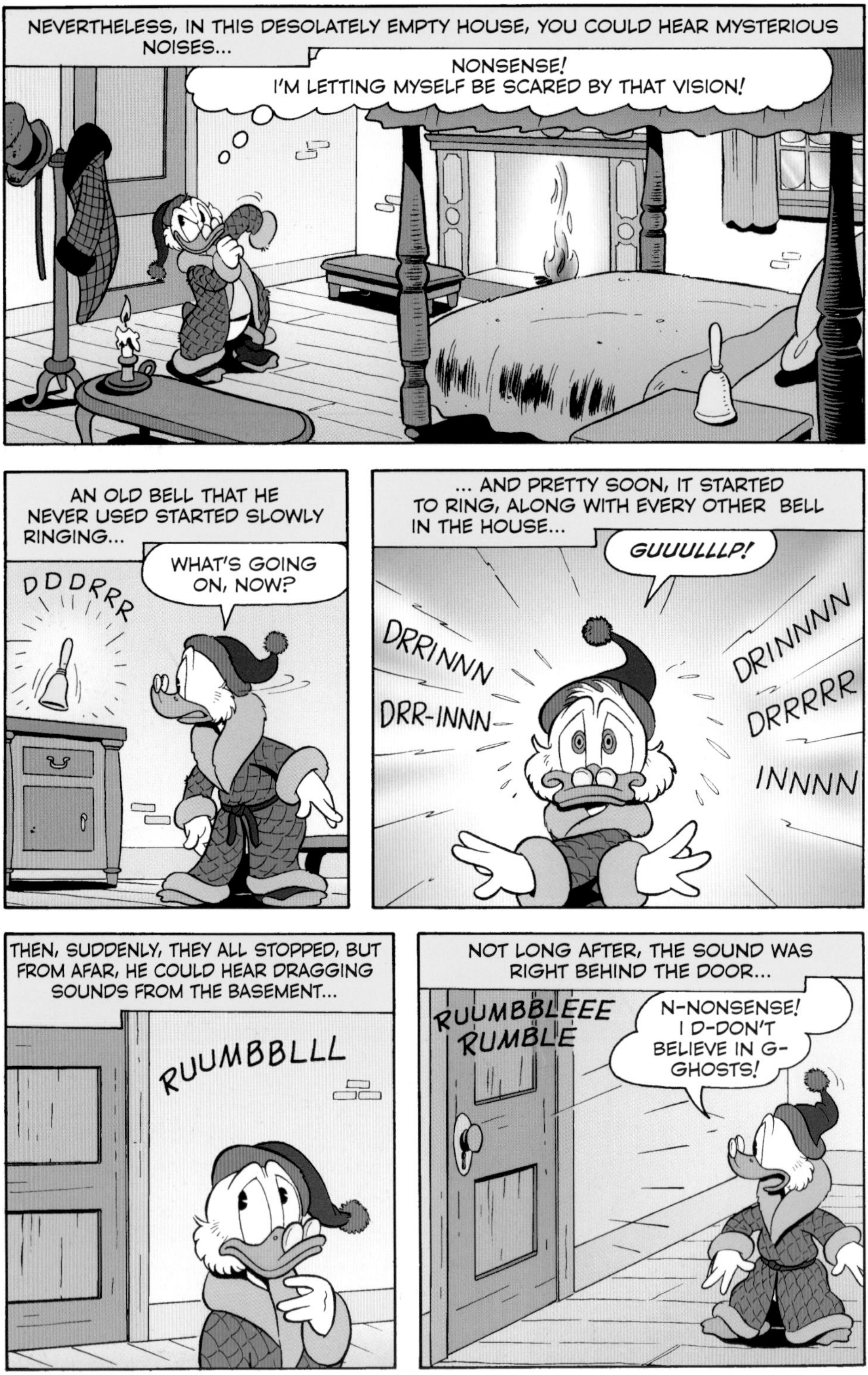
NEVERTHELESS, IN THIS DESOLATELY EMPTY HOUSE, YOU COULD HEAR MYSTERIOUS NOISES...
NONSENSE! I'M LETTING MYSELF BE SCARED BY THAT VISION!
AN OLD BELL THAT HE NEVER USED STARTED SLOWLY RINGING...
DDDRRRR
WHAT'S GOING ON, NOW?
... AND PRETTY SOON, IT STARTED TO RING, ALONG WITH EVERY OTHER BELL IN THE HOUSE...
GUUULLLP!
DRRINNN
DRR-INNN
DRINNNN
DRRRRR
INNNN
THEN, SUDDENLY, THEY ALL STOPPED, BUT FROM AFAR, HE COULD HEAR DRAGGING SOUNDS FROM THE BASEMENT...
RUUMBBLLL
NOT LONG AFTER, THE SOUND WAS RIGHT BEHIND THE DOOR...
RUUMBBLEEE RUMBLE
N-NONSENSE! I D-DON'T BELIEVE IN G-GHOSTS!

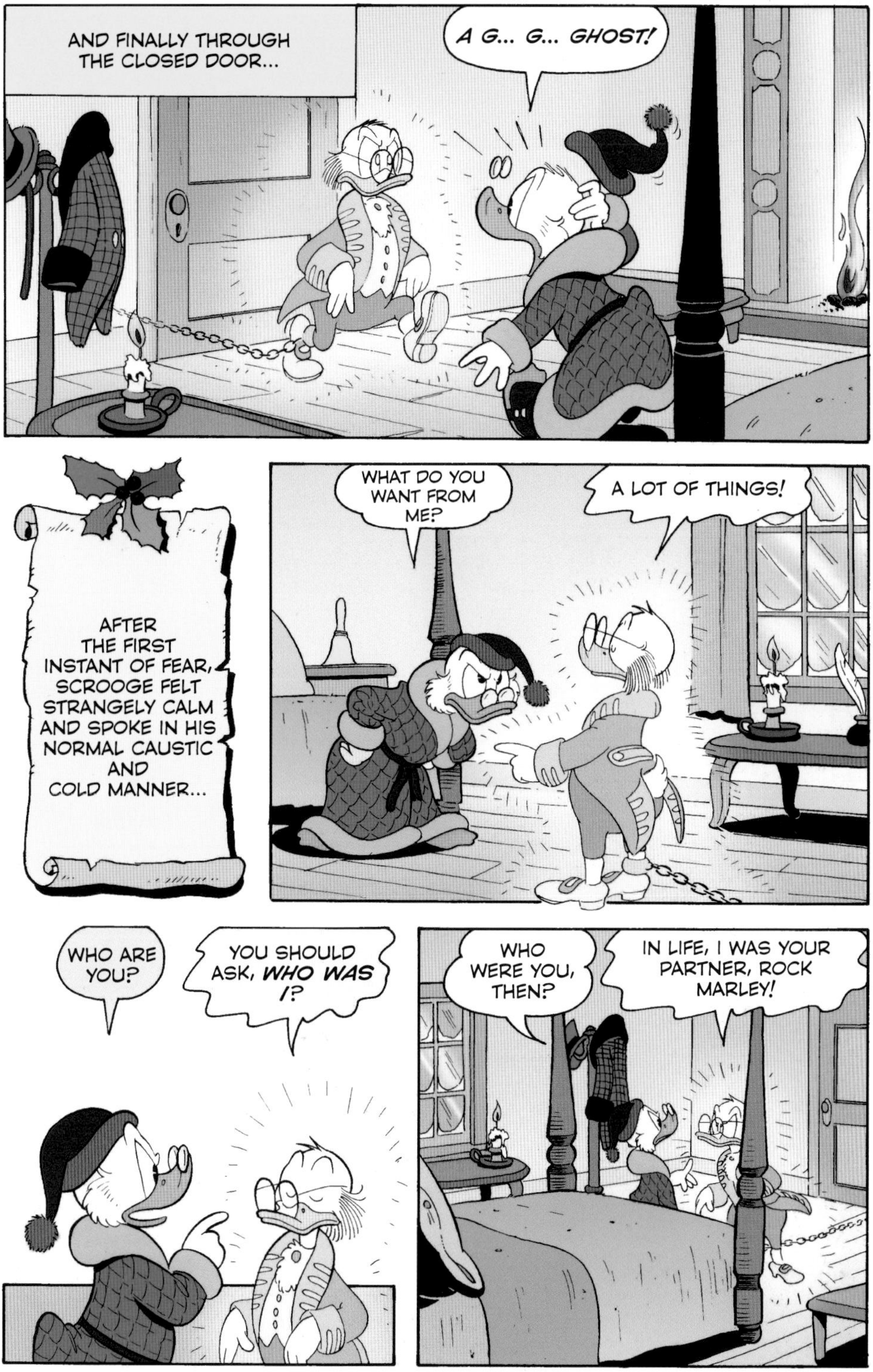

AND FINALLY THROUGH THE CLOSED DOOR...
A G... G... GHOST!
AFTER THE FIRST INSTANT OF FEAR, SCROOGE FELT STRANGELY CALM AND SPOKE IN HIS NORMAL CAUSTIC AND COLD MANNER...
WHAT DO YOU WANT FROM ME?
A LOT OF THINGS!
WHO ARE YOU?
YOU SHOULD ASK, ***WHO WAS I***?
WHO WERE YOU, THEN?
IN LIFE, I WAS YOUR PARTNER, ROCK MARLEY!

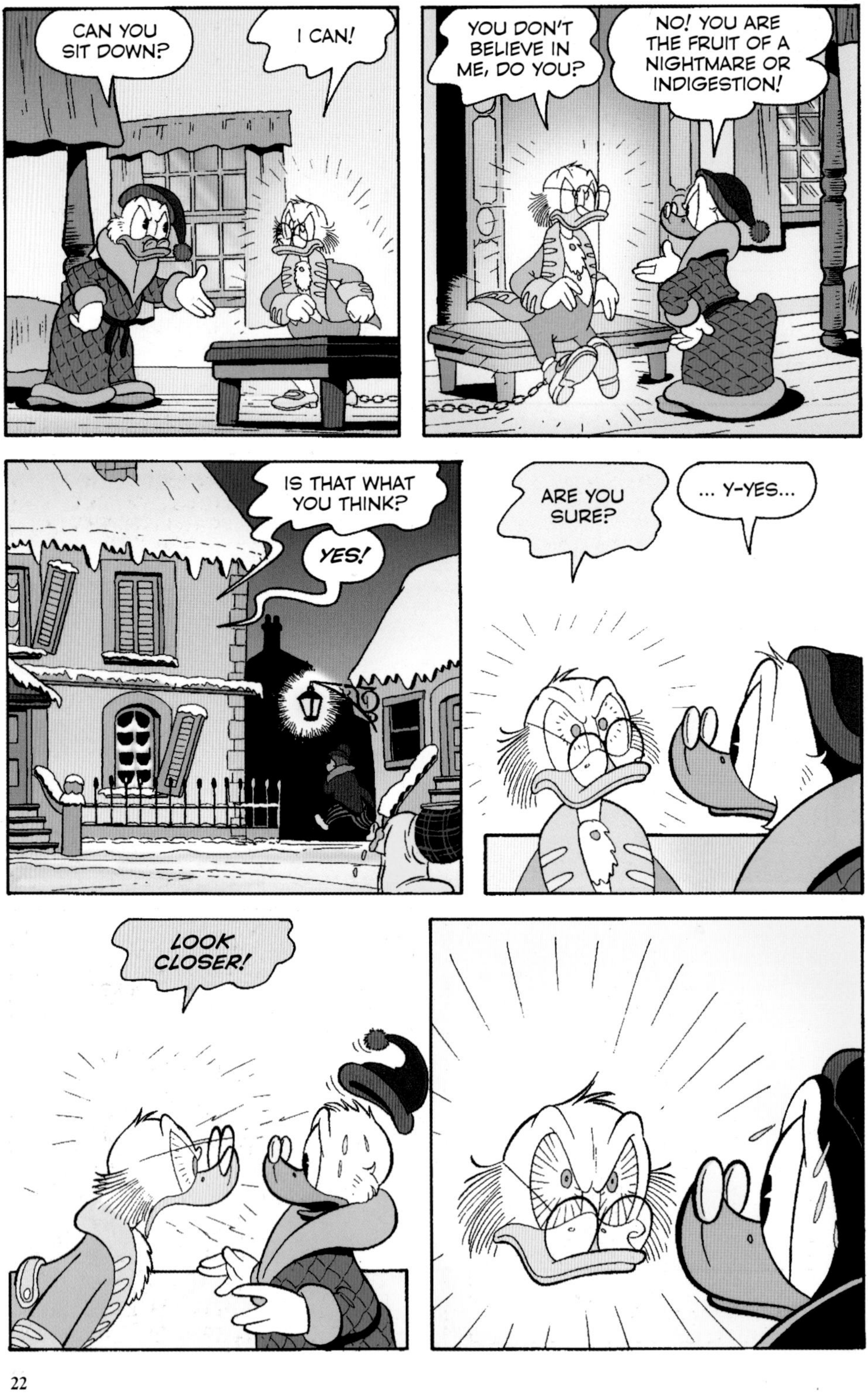
CAN YOU SIT DOWN?
I CAN!
YOU DON'T BELIEVE IN ME, DO YOU?
NO! YOU ARE THE FRUIT OF A NIGHTMARE OR INDIGESTION!
IS THAT WHAT YOU THINK?
YES!
ARE YOU SURE?
... Y-YES...
LOOK CLOSER!

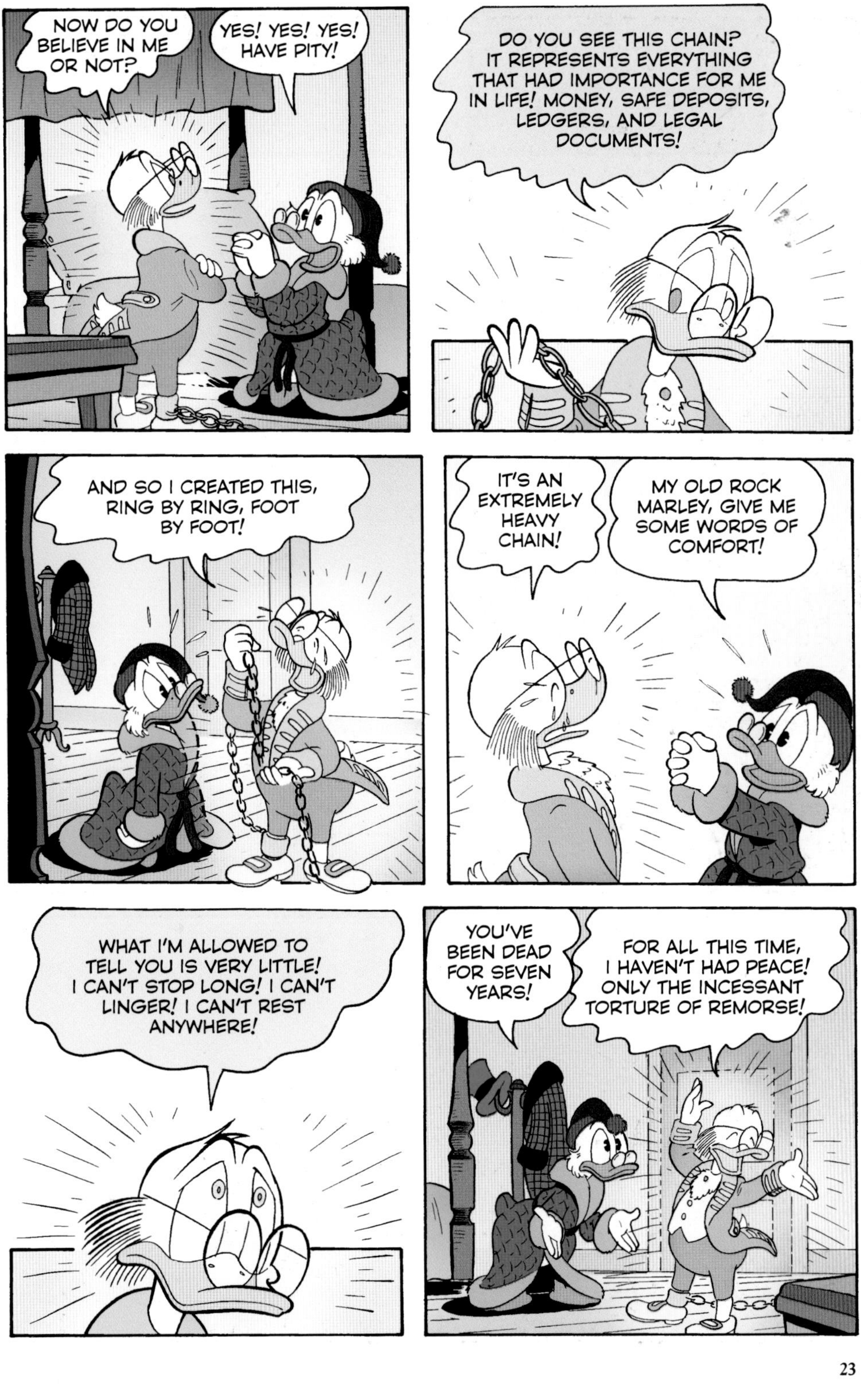
NOW DO YOU BELIEVE IN ME OR NOT?
YES! YES! YES! HAVE PITY!
DO YOU SEE THIS CHAIN? IT REPRESENTS EVERYTHING THAT HAD IMPORTANCE FOR ME IN LIFE! MONEY, SAFE DEPOSITS, LEDGERS, AND LEGAL DOCUMENTS!
AND SO I CREATED THIS, RING BY RING, FOOT BY FOOT!
IT'S AN EXTREMELY HEAVY CHAIN!
MY OLD ROCK MARLEY, GIVE ME SOME WORDS OF COMFORT!
WHAT I'M ALLOWED TO TELL YOU IS VERY LITTLE! I CAN'T STOP LONG! I CAN'T LINGER! I CAN'T REST ANYWHERE!
YOU'VE BEEN DEAD FOR SEVEN YEARS!
FOR ALL THIS TIME, I HAVEN'T HAD PEACE! ONLY THE INCESSANT TORTURE OF REMORSE!

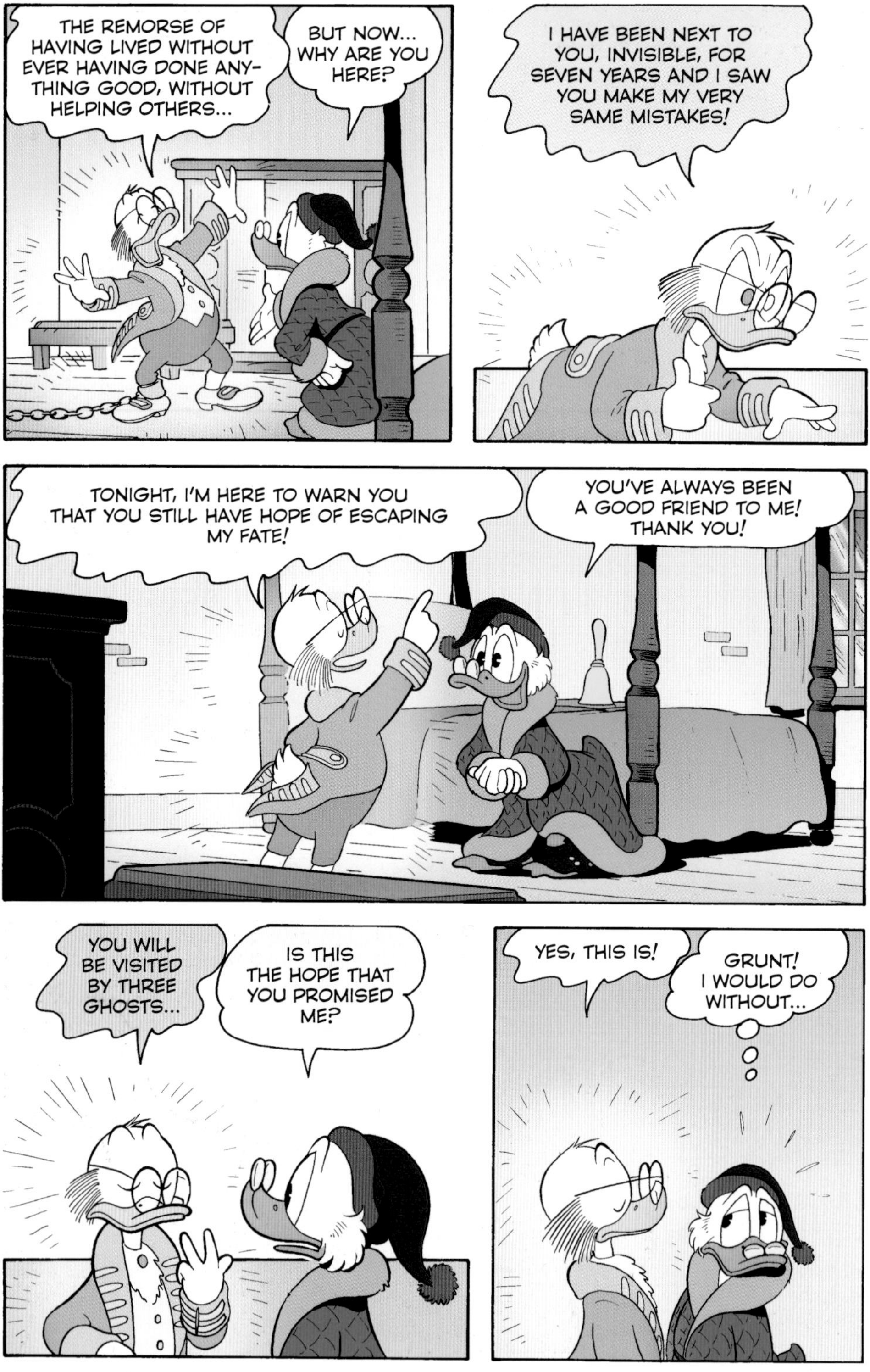

THE REMORSE OF HAVING LIVED WITHOUT EVER HAVING DONE ANY-THING GOOD, WITHOUT HELPING OTHERS...
BUT NOW... WHY ARE YOU HERE?
I HAVE BEEN NEXT TO YOU, INVISIBLE, FOR SEVEN YEARS AND I SAW YOU MAKE MY VERY SAME MISTAKES!
TONIGHT, I'M HERE TO WARN YOU THAT YOU STILL HAVE HOPE OF ESCAPING MY FATE!
YOU'VE ALWAYS BEEN A GOOD FRIEND TO ME! THANK YOU!
YOU WILL BE VISITED BY THREE GHOSTS...
IS THIS THE HOPE THAT YOU PROMISED ME?
YES, THIS IS!
GRUNT! I WOULD DO WITHOUT...

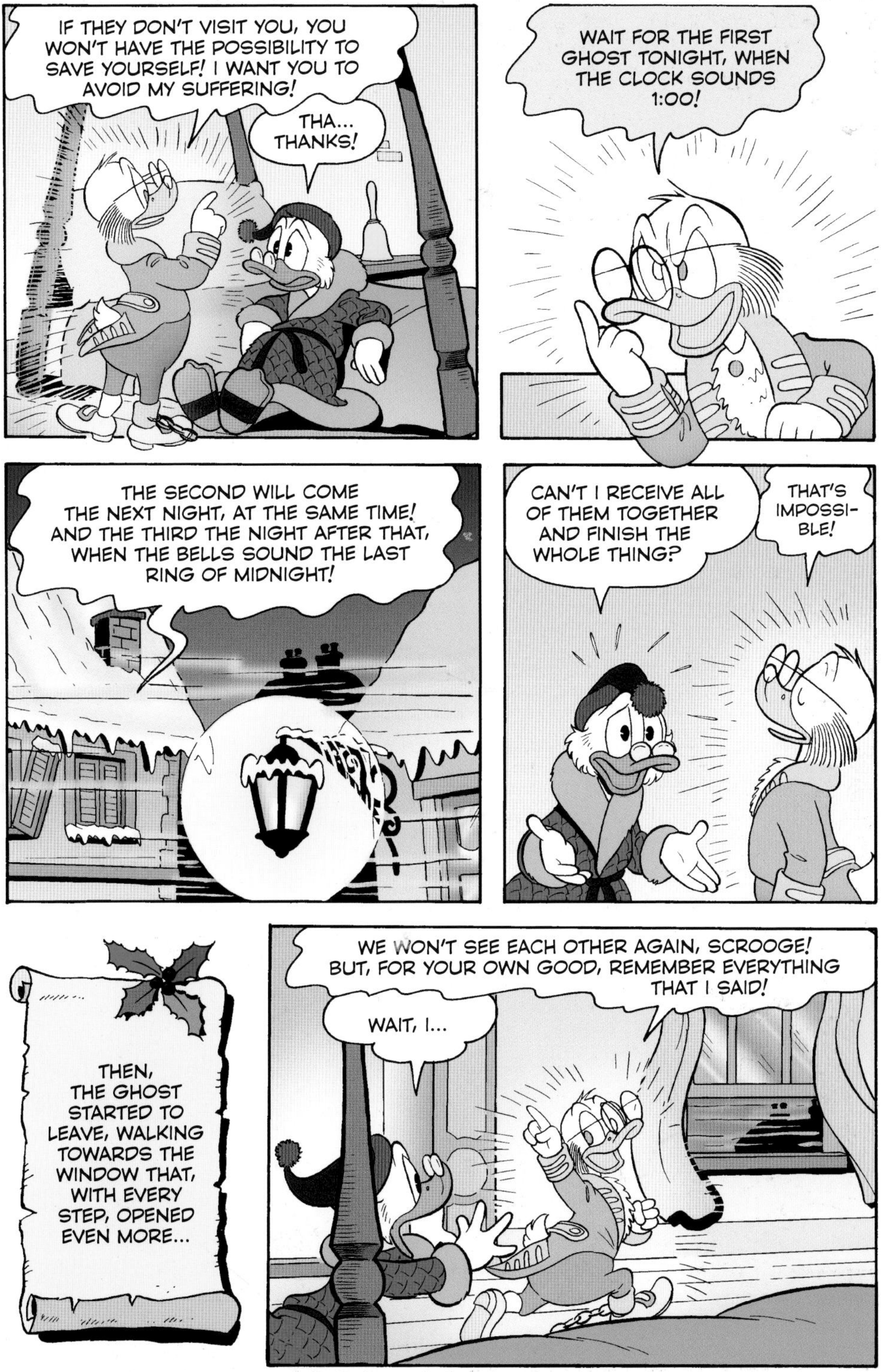
IF THEY DON'T VISIT YOU, YOU WON'T HAVE THE POSSIBILITY TO SAVE YOURSELF! I WANT YOU TO AVOID MY SUFFERING!
THA... THANKS!
WAIT FOR THE FIRST GHOST TONIGHT, WHEN THE CLOCK SOUNDS 1:00!
THE SECOND WILL COME THE NEXT NIGHT, AT THE SAME TIME! AND THE THIRD THE NIGHT AFTER THAT, WHEN THE BELLS SOUND THE LAST RING OF MIDNIGHT!
CAN'T I RECEIVE ALL OF THEM TOGETHER AND FINISH THE WHOLE THING?
THAT'S IMPOSSI-BLE!
THEN, THE GHOST STARTED TO LEAVE, WALKING TOWARDS THE WINDOW THAT, WITH EVERY STEP, OPENED EVEN MORE...
WE WON'T SEE EACH OTHER AGAIN, SCROOGE! BUT, FOR YOUR OWN GOOD, REMEMBER EVERYTHING THAT I SAID!
WAIT, I...

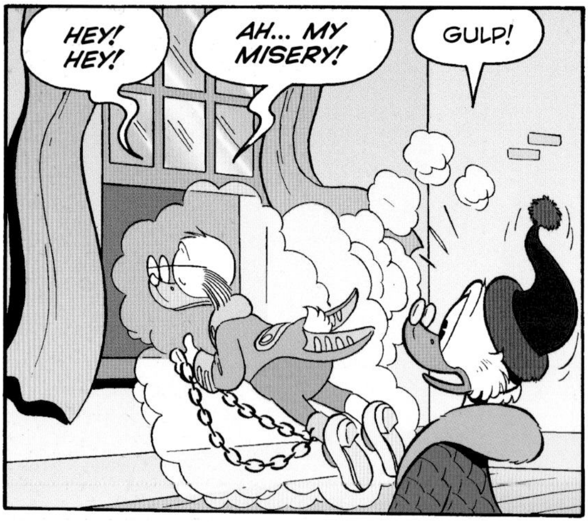
HEY! HEY!
AH... MY MISERY!
GULP!

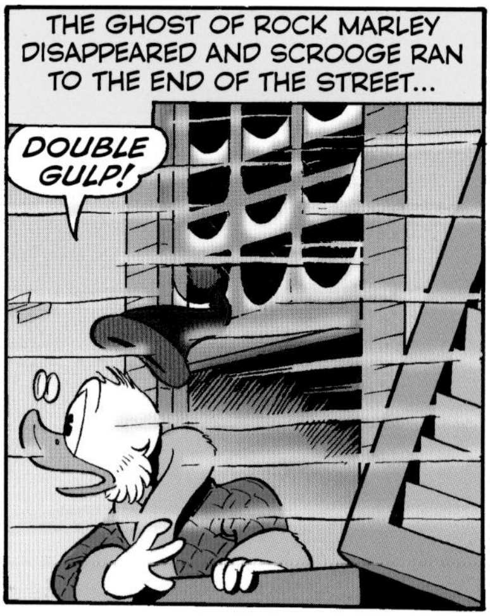
THE GHOST OF ROCK MARLEY DISAPPEARED AND SCROOGE RAN TO THE END OF THE STREET...
DOUBLE GULP!

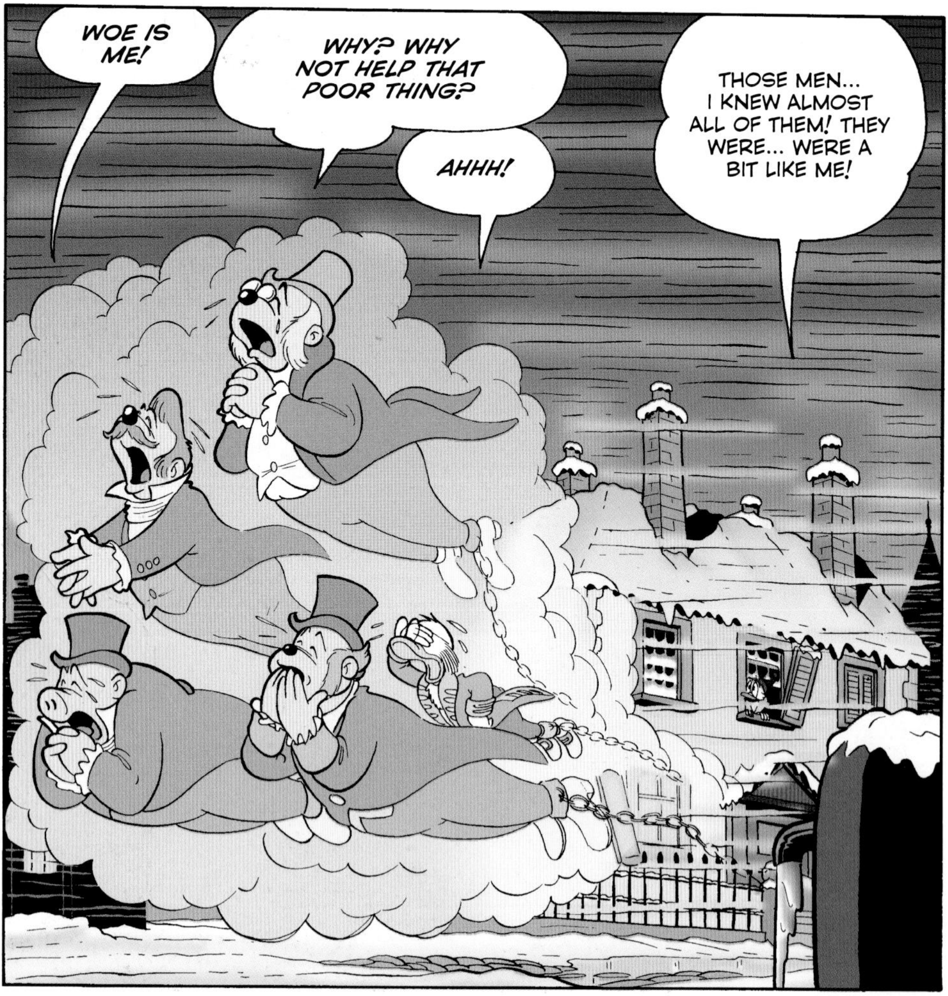
WOE IS ME!
WHY? WHY NOT HELP THAT POOR THING?
AHHH!
THOSE MEN... I KNEW ALMOST ALL OF THEM! THEY WERE... WERE A BIT LIKE ME!

THEN, EVERYTHING TURNED BACK TO NORMAL...

THE FOG SWAL-LOWED THEM ALL!

OR WAS IT ONLY FOG THAT I SAW?

NONSENSE! ONLY NONSENSE!

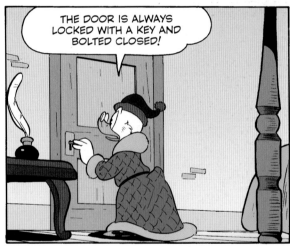

THE DOOR IS ALWAYS LOCKED WITH A KEY AND BOLTED CLOSED!

THERE WAS SO MUCH NONSENSE THAT SCROOGE WENT TO BED WITHOUT UNDRESSING AND FELL INTO A DEEP SLEEP...

YES, ONLY NONSENSE, AND I REALLY NEED MY REST! I AM WORN... ZZZ... ZZZZ...

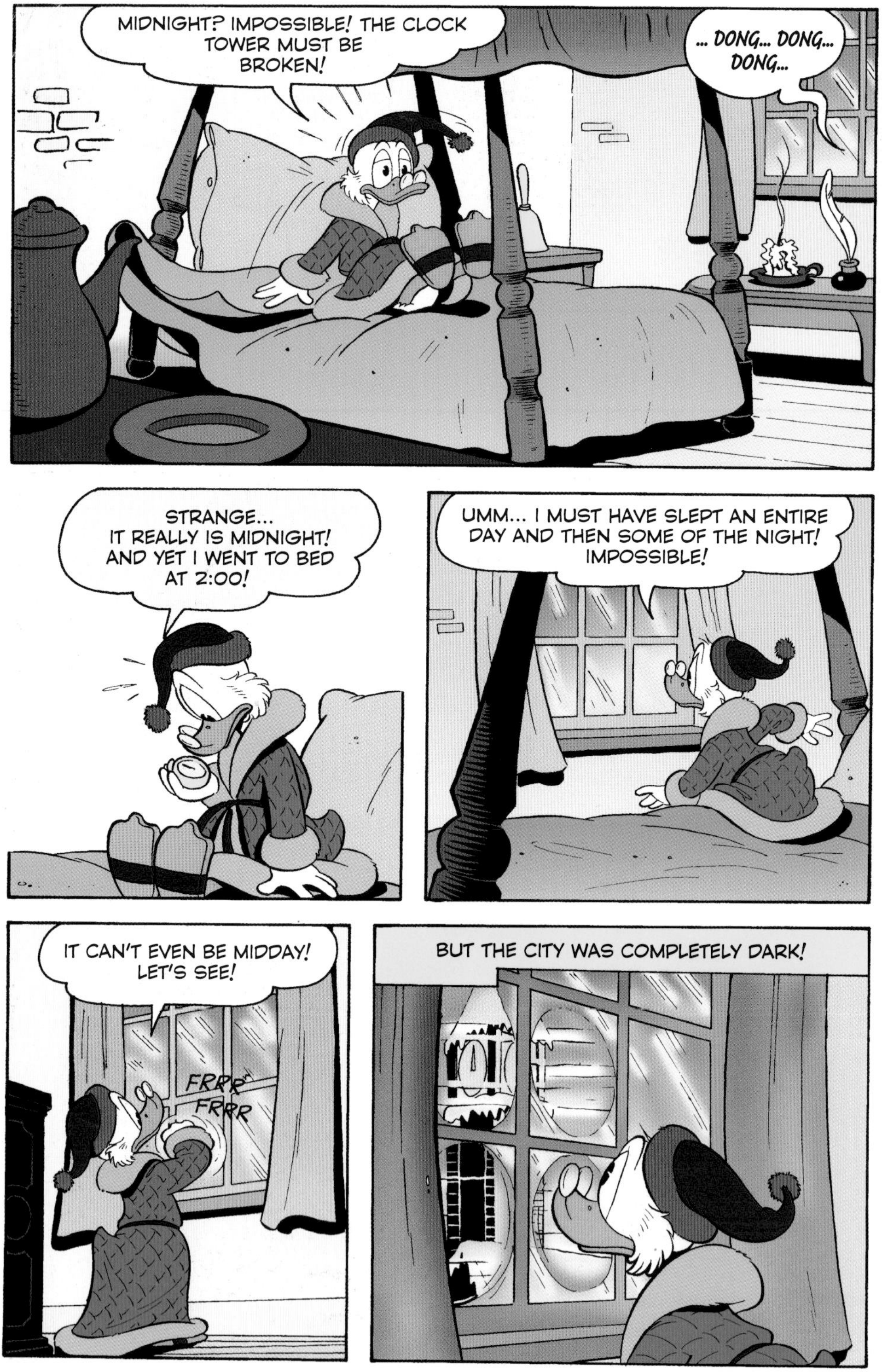
MIDNIGHT? IMPOSSIBLE! THE CLOCK TOWER MUST BE BROKEN!
... DONG... DONG... DONG...
STRANGE... IT REALLY IS MIDNIGHT! AND YET I WENT TO BED AT 2:00!
UMM... I MUST HAVE SLEPT AN ENTIRE DAY AND THEN SOME OF THE NIGHT! IMPOSSIBLE!
IT CAN'T EVEN BE MIDDAY! LET'S SEE!
FRRR FRRR
BUT THE CITY WAS COMPLETELY DARK!

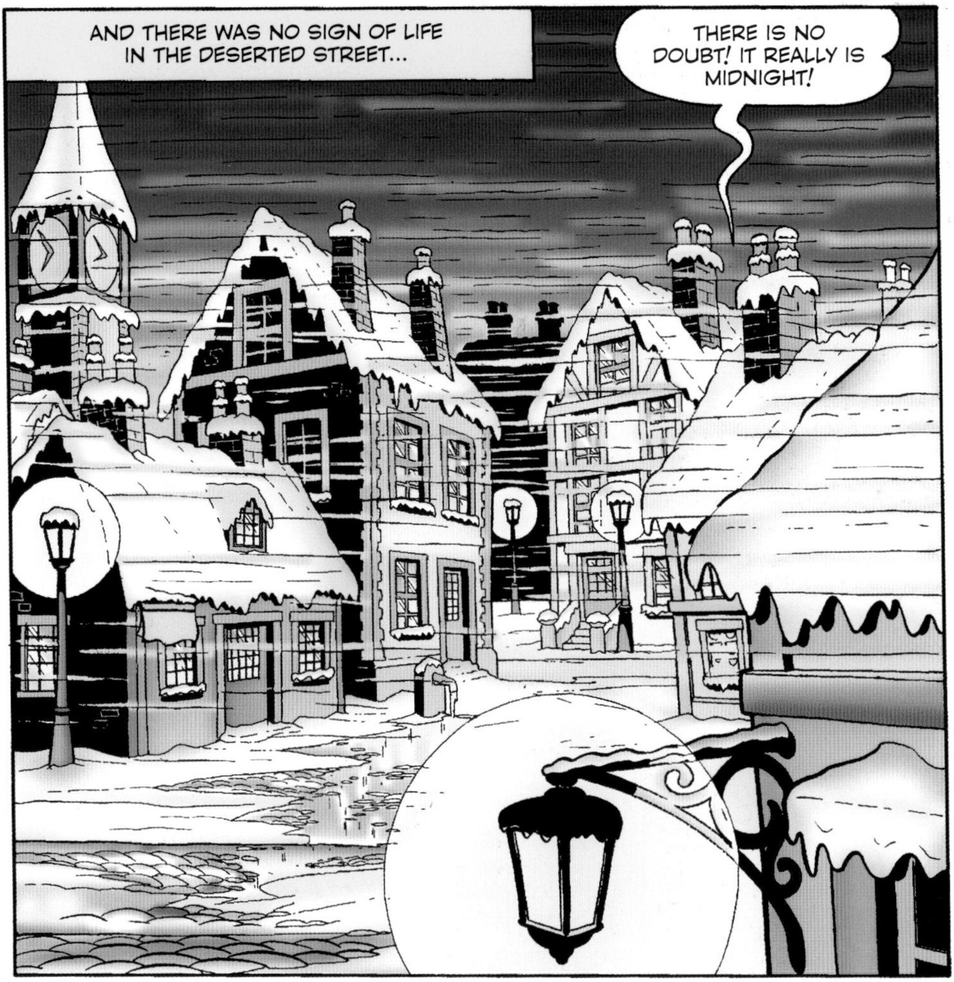
AND THERE WAS NO SIGN OF LIFE IN THE DESERTED STREET...
THERE IS NO DOUBT! IT REALLY IS MIDNIGHT!

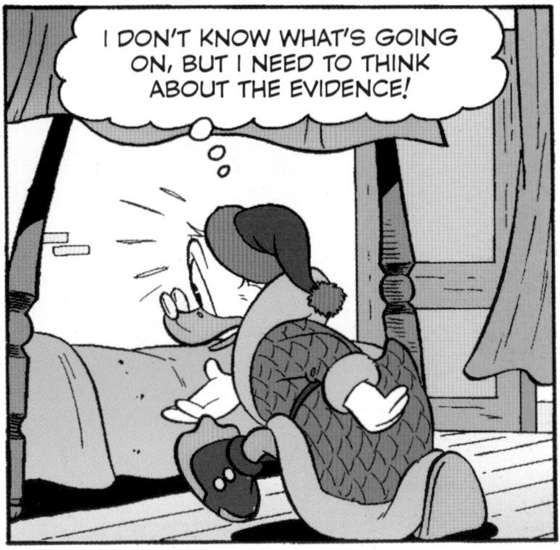
I DON'T KNOW WHAT'S GOING ON, BUT I NEED TO THINK ABOUT THE EVIDENCE!

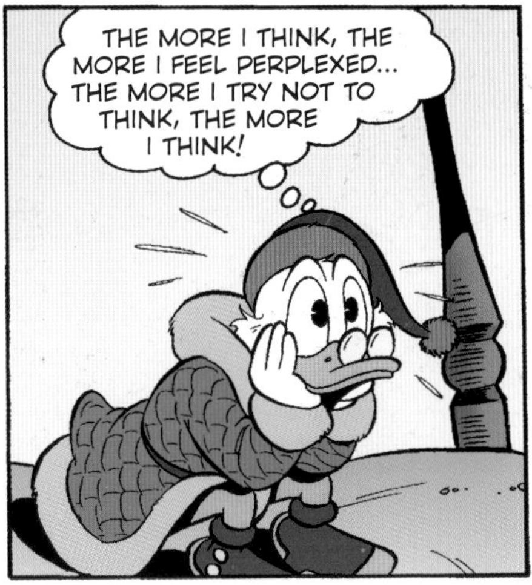
THE MORE I THINK, THE MORE I FEEL PERPLEXED... THE MORE I TRY NOT TO THINK, THE MORE I THINK!

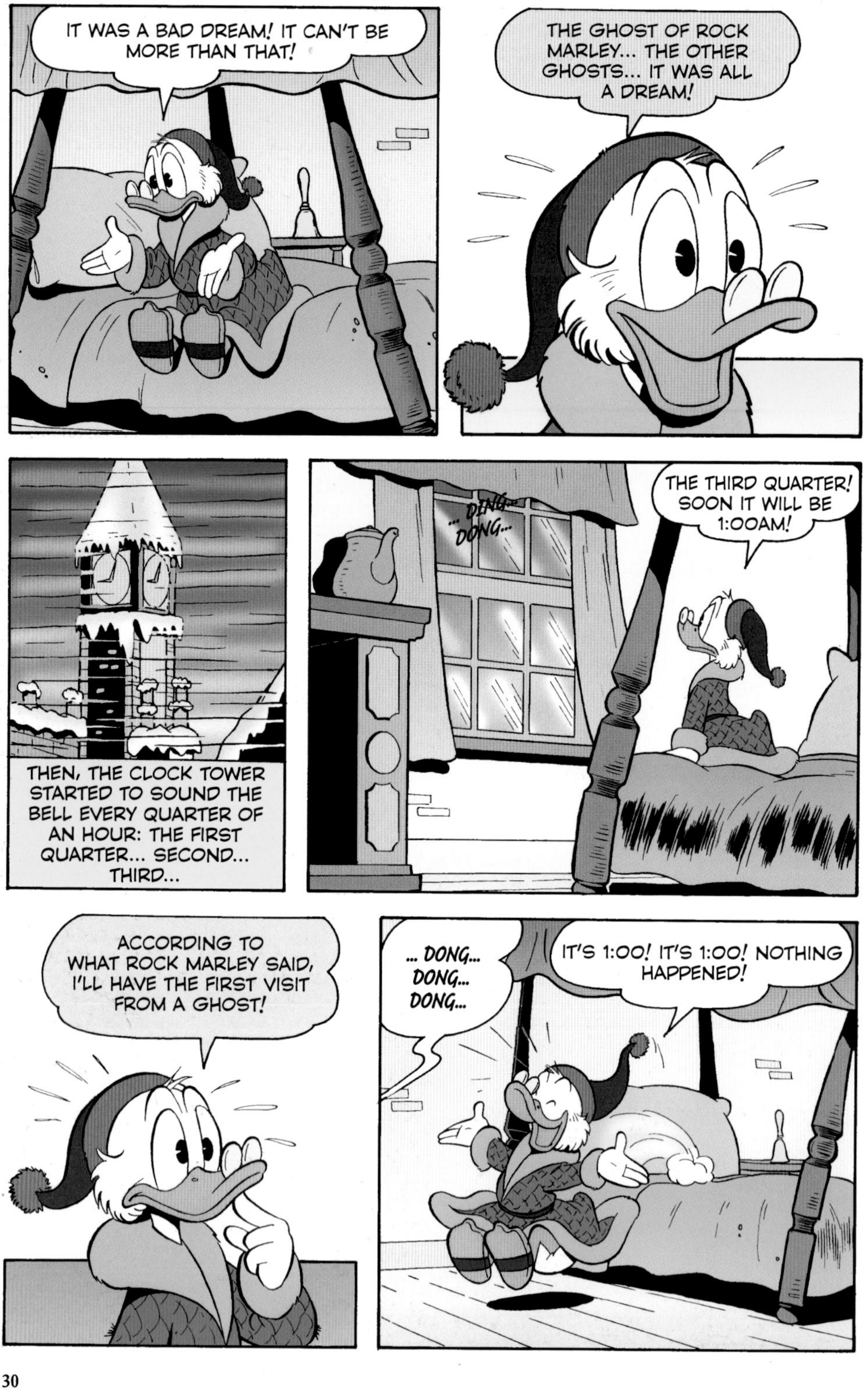
IT WAS A BAD DREAM! IT CAN'T BE MORE THAN THAT!
THE GHOST OF ROCK MARLEY... THE OTHER GHOSTS... IT WAS ALL A DREAM!
THEN, THE CLOCK TOWER STARTED TO SOUND THE BELL EVERY QUARTER OF AN HOUR: THE FIRST QUARTER... SECOND... THIRD...
... DING... DONG...
THE THIRD QUARTER! SOON IT WILL BE 1:00AM!
ACCORDING TO WHAT ROCK MARLEY SAID, I'LL HAVE THE FIRST VISIT FROM A GHOST!
... DONG... DONG... DONG...
IT'S 1:00! IT'S 1:00! NOTHING HAPPENED!

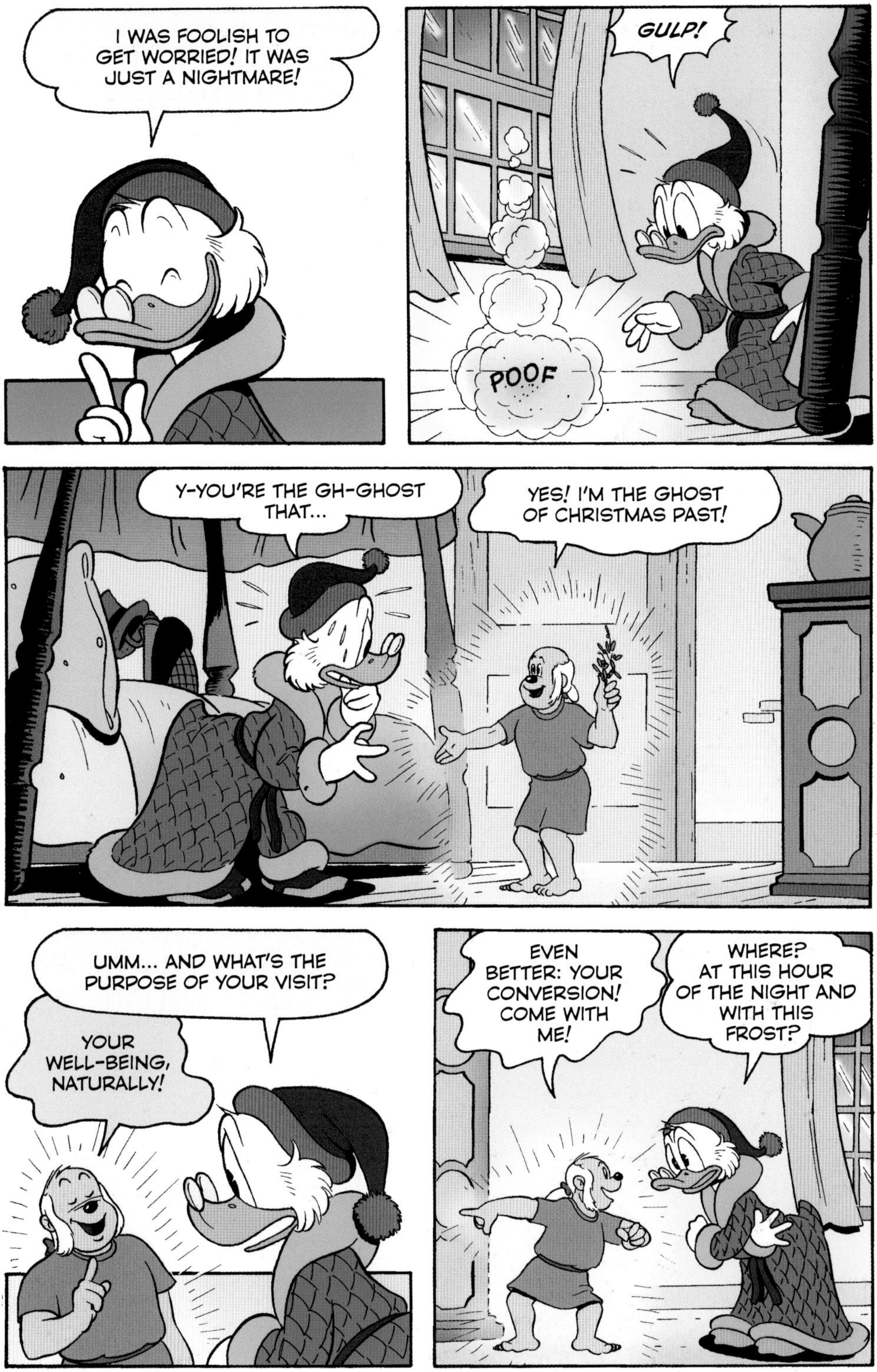
I WAS FOOLISH TO GET WORRIED! IT WAS JUST A NIGHTMARE!
GULP!
POOF
Y-YOU'RE THE GH-GHOST THAT...
YES! I'M THE GHOST OF CHRISTMAS PAST!
UMM... AND WHAT'S THE PURPOSE OF YOUR VISIT?
YOUR WELL-BEING, NATURALLY!
EVEN BETTER: YOUR CONVERSION! COME WITH ME!
WHERE? AT THIS HOUR OF THE NIGHT AND WITH THIS FROST?

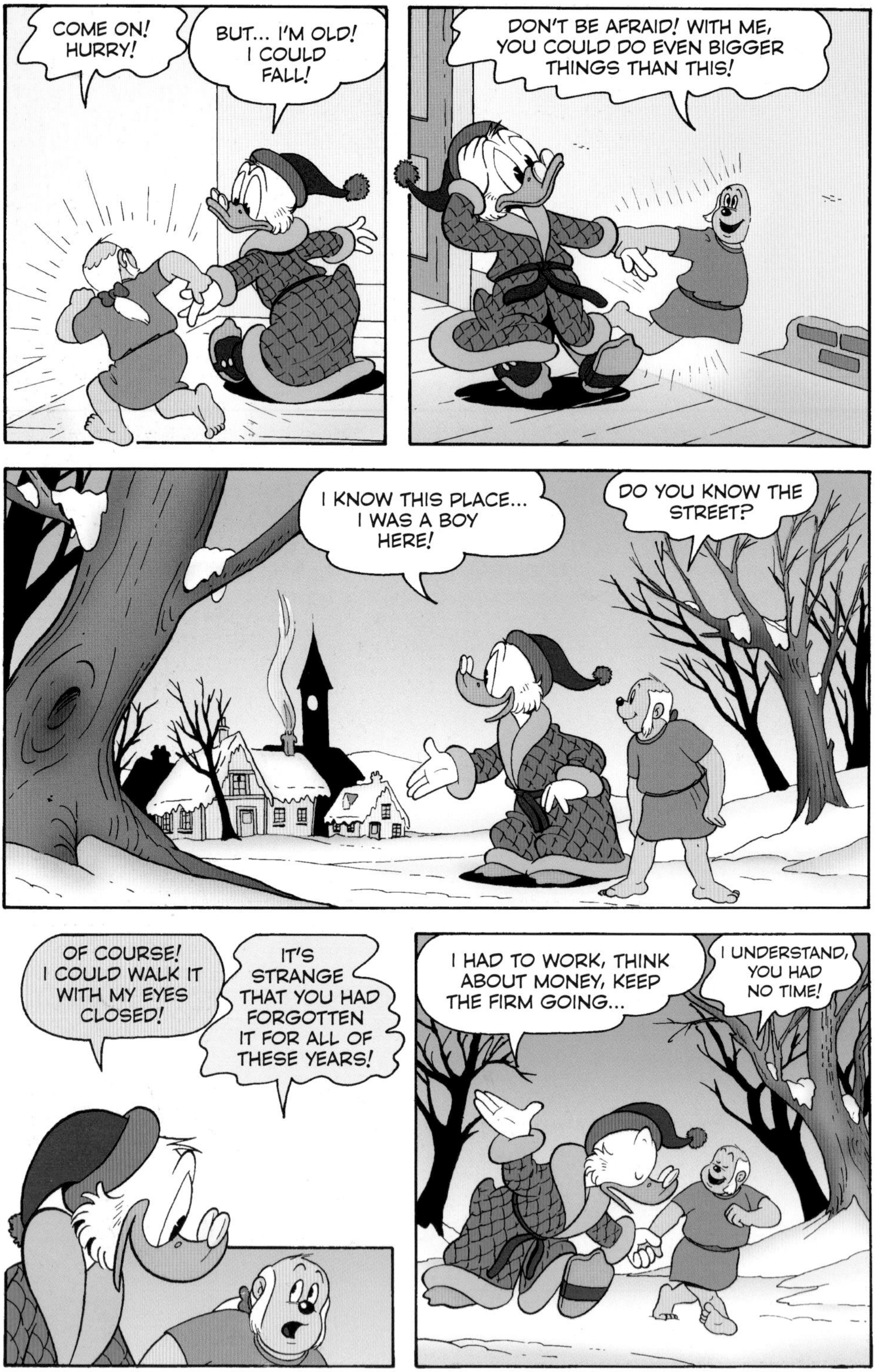
COME ON! HURRY!
BUT... I'M OLD! I COULD FALL!
DON'T BE AFRAID! WITH ME, YOU COULD DO EVEN BIGGER THINGS THAN THIS!
I KNOW THIS PLACE... I WAS A BOY HERE!
DO YOU KNOW THE STREET?
OF COURSE! I COULD WALK IT WITH MY EYES CLOSED!
IT'S STRANGE THAT YOU HAD FORGOTTEN IT FOR ALL OF THESE YEARS!
I HAD TO WORK, THINK ABOUT MONEY, KEEP THE FIRM GOING...
I UNDERSTAND, YOU HAD NO TIME!

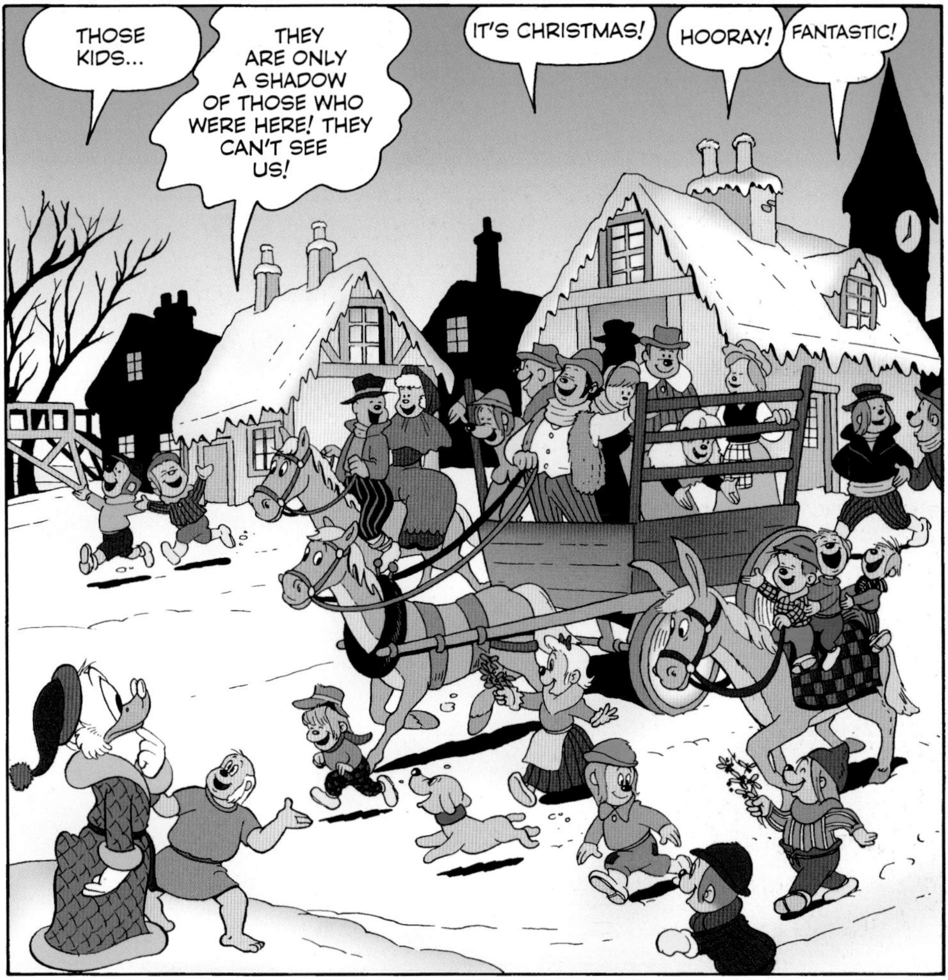
THOSE KIDS...
THEY ARE ONLY A SHADOW OF THOSE WHO WERE HERE! THEY CAN'T SEE US!
IT'S CHRISTMAS!
HOORAY!
FANTASTIC!

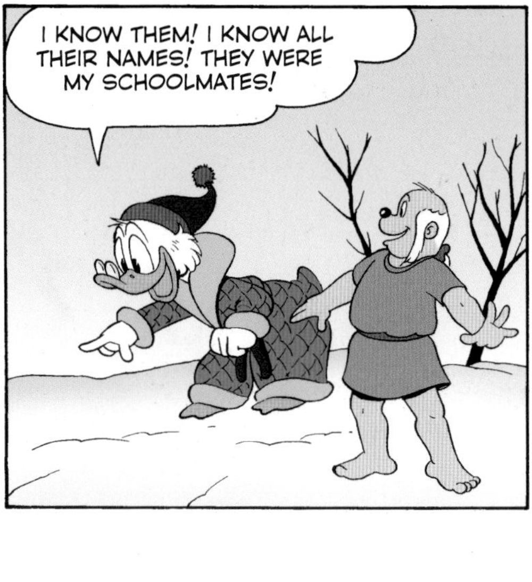
I KNOW THEM! I KNOW ALL THEIR NAMES! THEY WERE MY SCHOOLMATES!

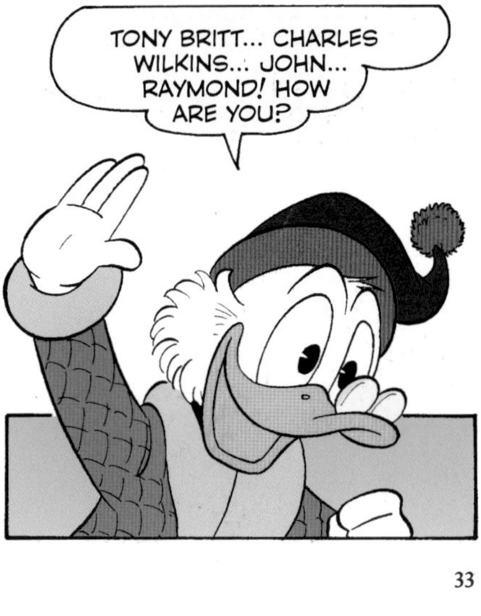
TONY BRITT... CHARLES WILKINS... JOHN... RAYMOND! HOW ARE YOU?

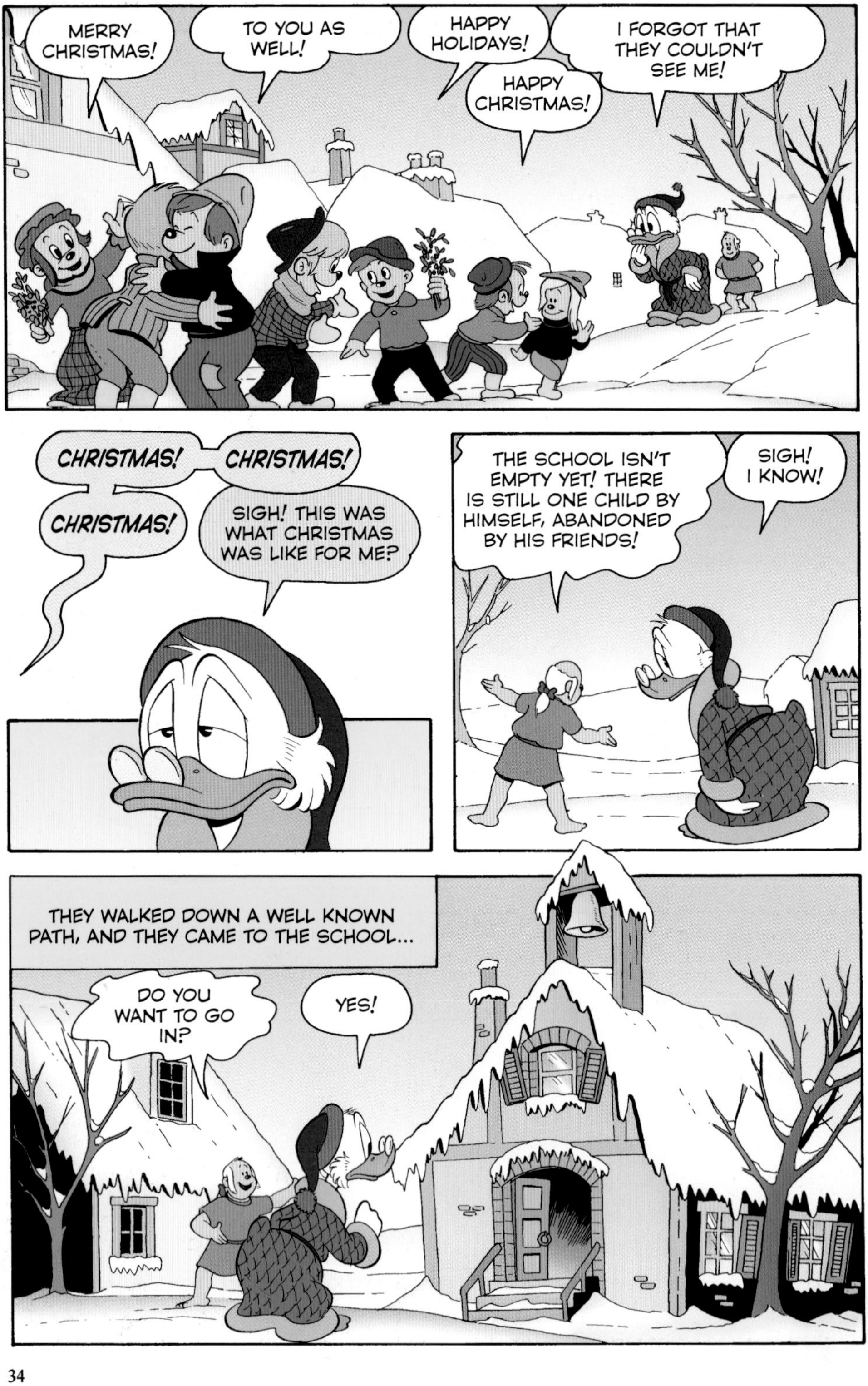
MERRY CHRISTMAS!
TO YOU AS WELL!
HAPPY HOLIDAYS!
HAPPY CHRISTMAS!
I FORGOT THAT THEY COULDN'T SEE ME!
CHRISTMAS!
CHRISTMAS!
CHRISTMAS!
SIGH! THIS WAS WHAT CHRISTMAS WAS LIKE FOR ME?
THE SCHOOL ISN'T EMPTY YET! THERE IS STILL ONE CHILD BY HIMSELF, ABANDONED BY HIS FRIENDS!
SIGH! I KNOW!
THEY WALKED DOWN A WELL KNOWN PATH, AND THEY CAME TO THE SCHOOL...
DO YOU WANT TO GO IN?
YES!

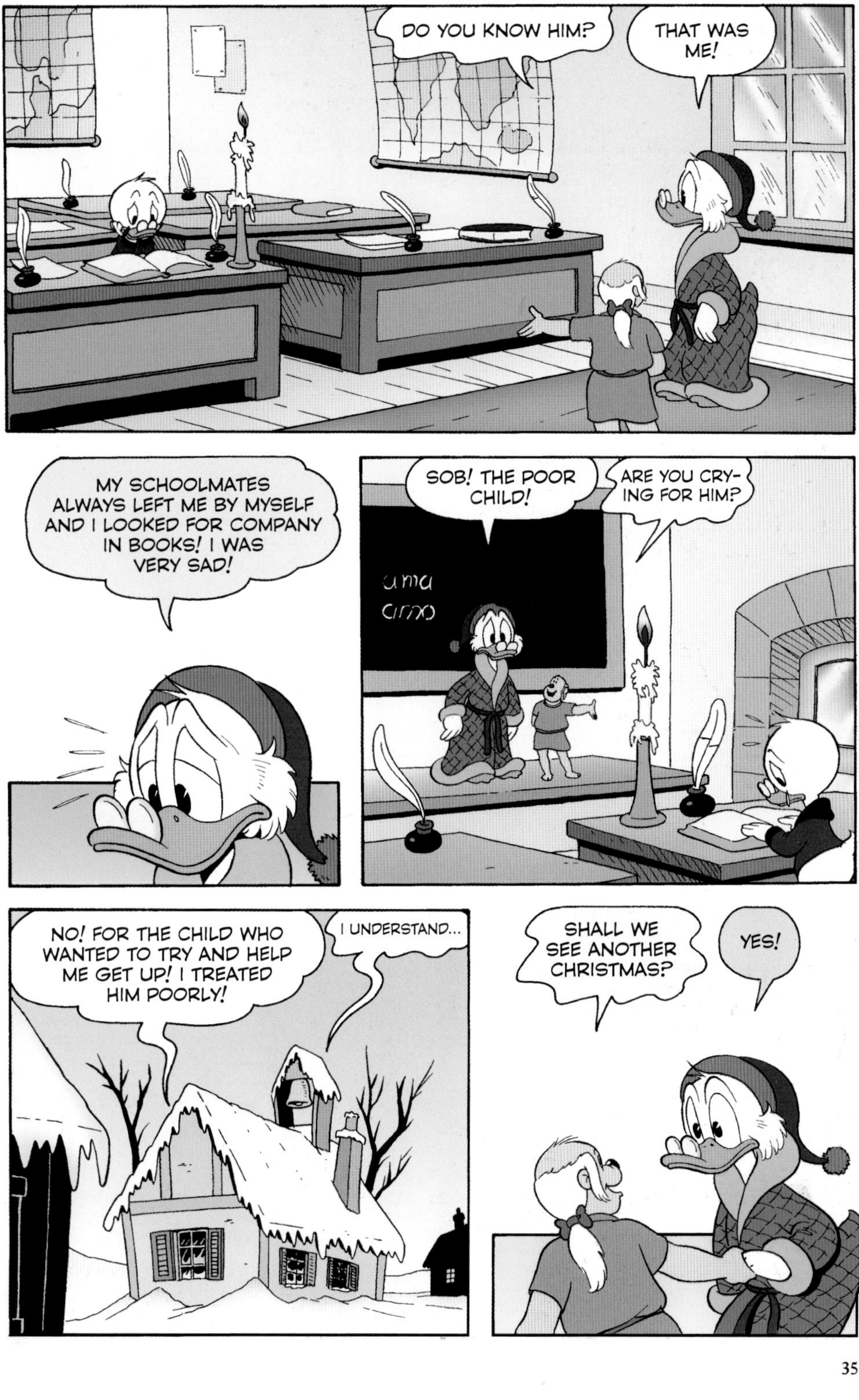
DO YOU KNOW HIM?
THAT WAS ME!
MY SCHOOLMATES ALWAYS LEFT ME BY MYSELF AND I LOOKED FOR COMPANY IN BOOKS! I WAS VERY SAD!
SOB! THE POOR CHILD!
ARE YOU CRY-ING FOR HIM?
NO! FOR THE CHILD WHO WANTED TO TRY AND HELP ME GET UP! I TREATED HIM POORLY!
I UNDERSTAND...
SHALL WE SEE ANOTHER CHRISTMAS?
YES!

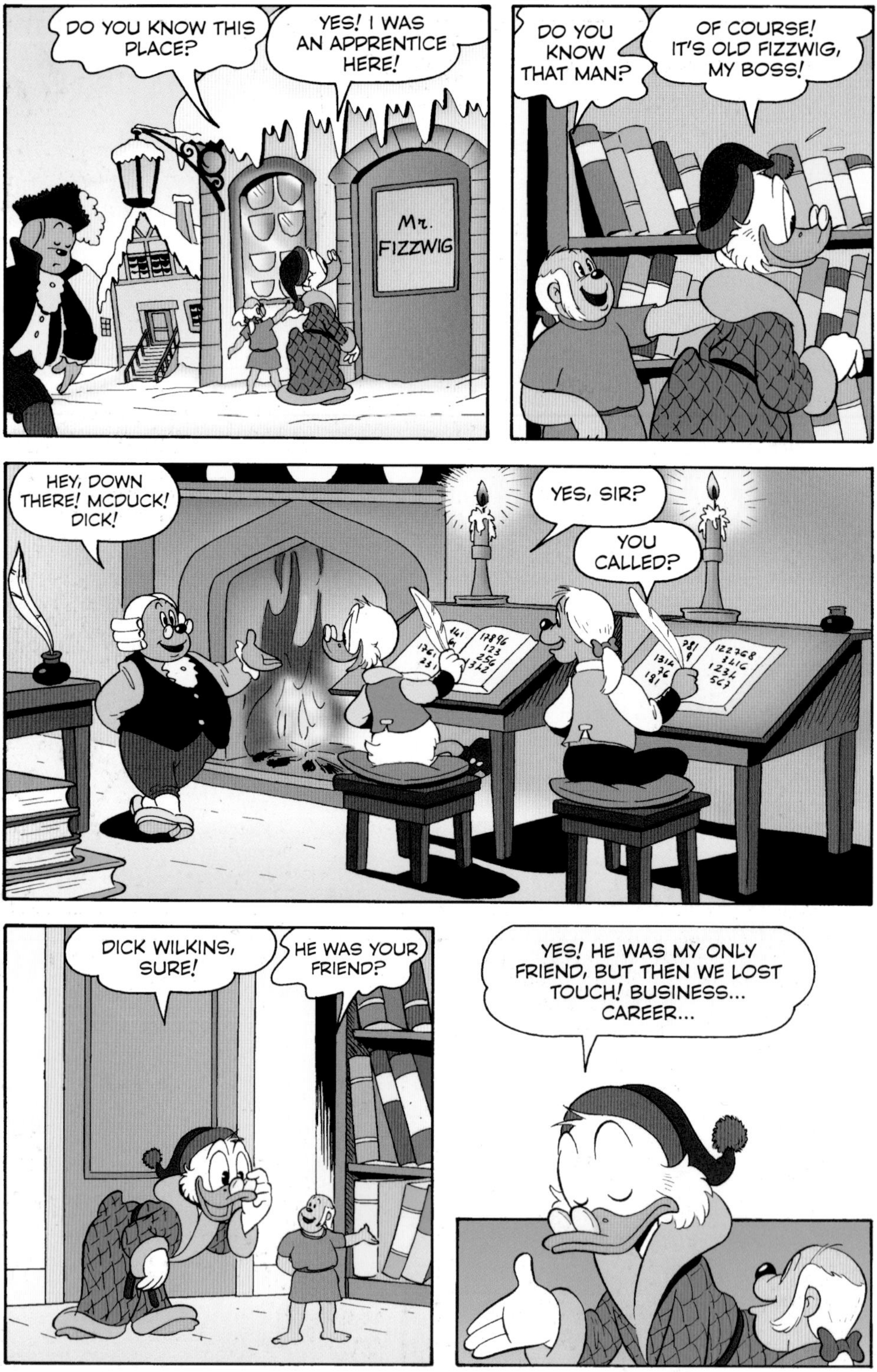
DO YOU KNOW THIS PLACE?
YES! I WAS AN APPRENTICE HERE!
Mr. FIZZWIG
DO YOU KNOW THAT MAN?
OF COURSE! IT'S OLD FIZZWIG, MY BOSS!
HEY, DOWN THERE! MCDUCK! DICK!
YES, SIR?
YOU CALLED?
DICK WILKINS, SURE!
HE WAS YOUR FRIEND?
YES! HE WAS MY ONLY FRIEND, BUT THEN WE LOST TOUCH! BUSINESS... CAREER...

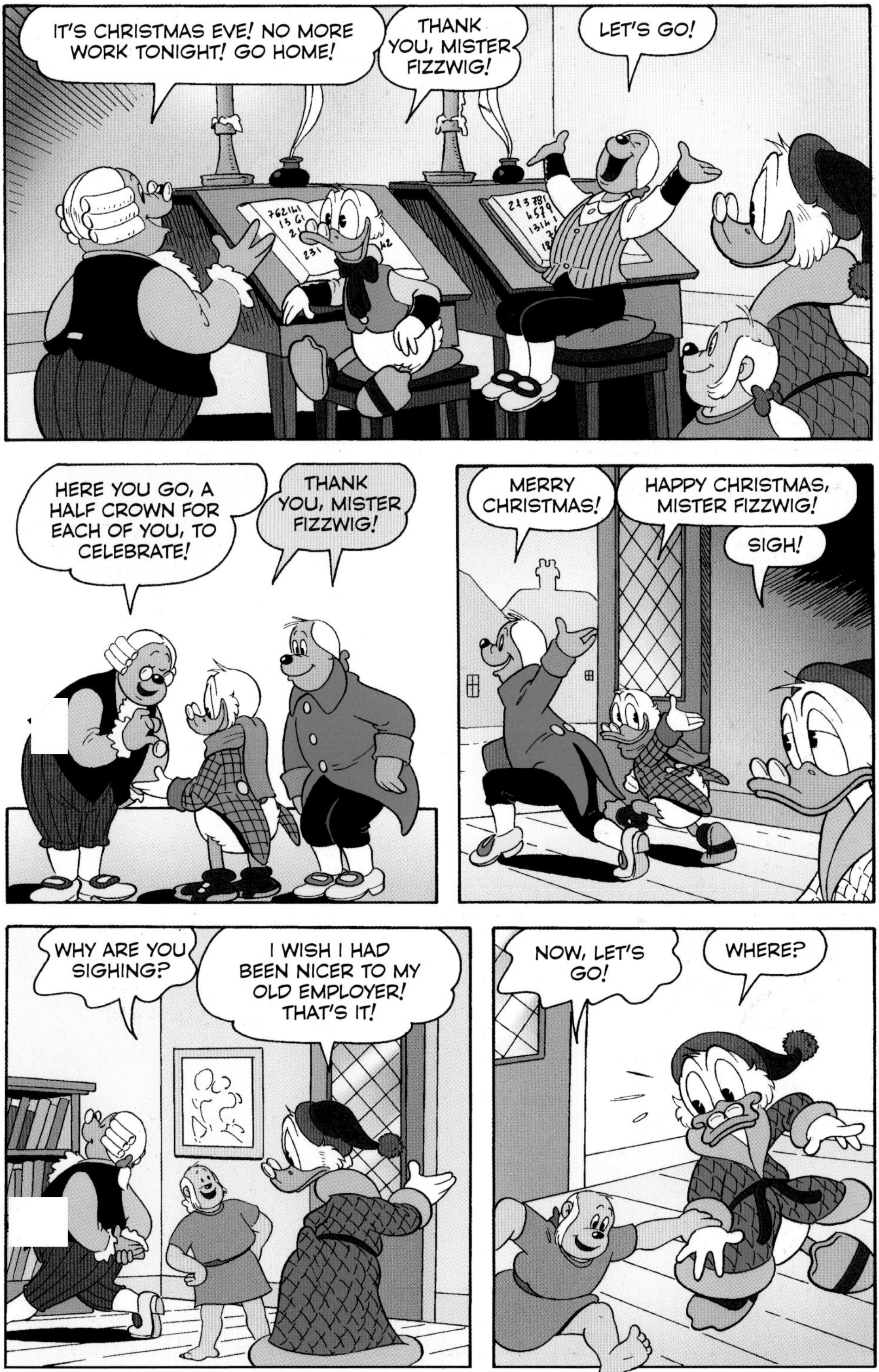
IT'S CHRISTMAS EVE! NO MORE WORK TONIGHT! GO HOME!
THANK YOU, MISTER FIZZWIG!
LET'S GO!
HERE YOU GO, A HALF CROWN FOR EACH OF YOU, TO CELEBRATE!
THANK YOU, MISTER FIZZWIG!
MERRY CHRISTMAS!
HAPPY CHRISTMAS, MISTER FIZZWIG!
SIGH!
WHY ARE YOU SIGHING?
I WISH I HAD BEEN NICER TO MY OLD EMPLOYER! THAT'S IT!
NOW, LET'S GO!
WHERE?

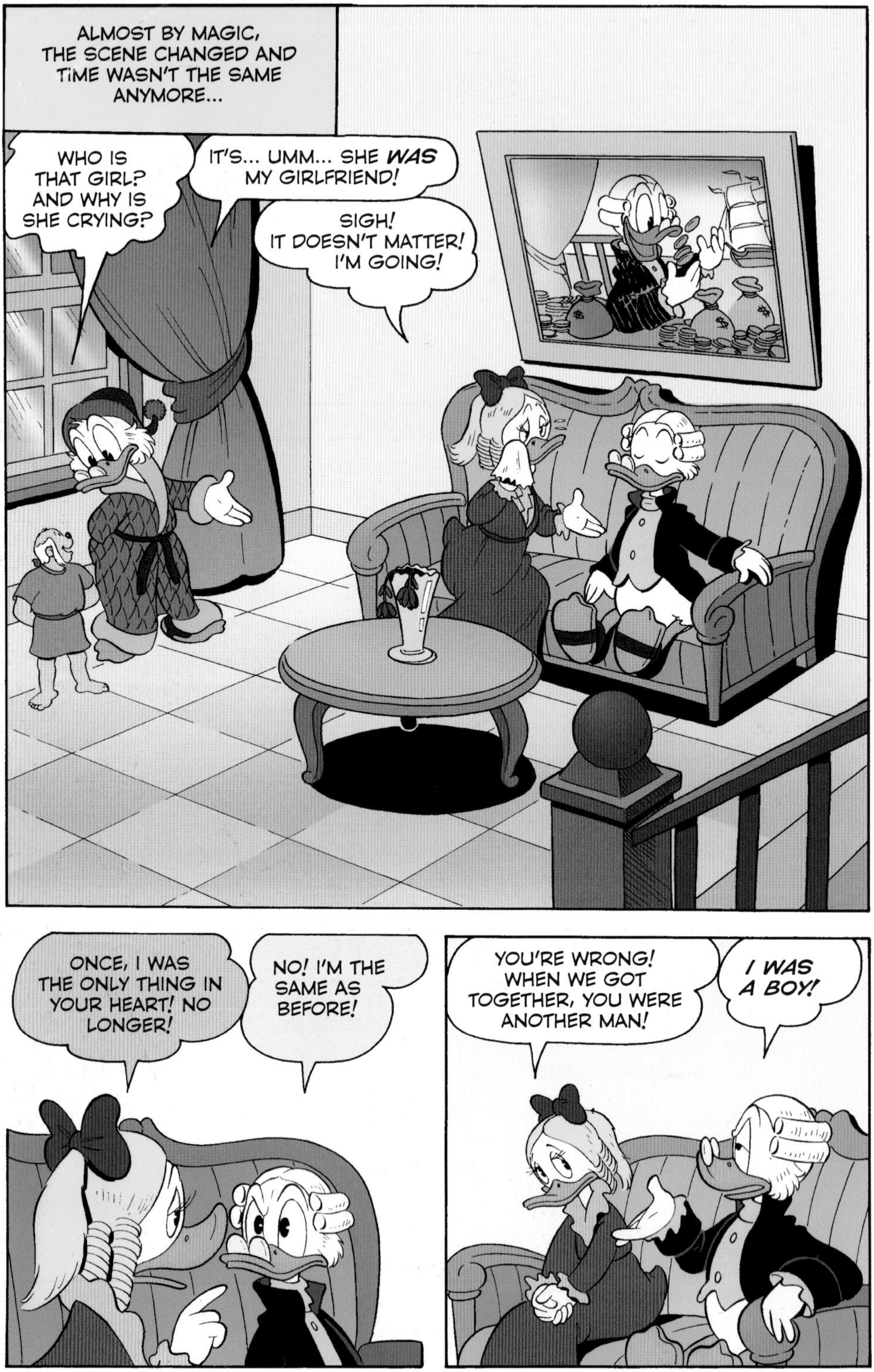
ALMOST BY MAGIC, THE SCENE CHANGED AND TIME WASN'T THE SAME ANYMORE...
WHO IS THAT GIRL? AND WHY IS SHE CRYING?
IT'S... UMM... SHE *WAS* MY GIRLFRIEND!
SIGH! IT DOESN'T MATTER! I'M GOING!
ONCE, I WAS THE ONLY THING IN YOUR HEART! NO LONGER!
NO! I'M THE SAME AS BEFORE!
YOU'RE WRONG! WHEN WE GOT TOGETHER, YOU WERE ANOTHER MAN!
I WAS A BOY!

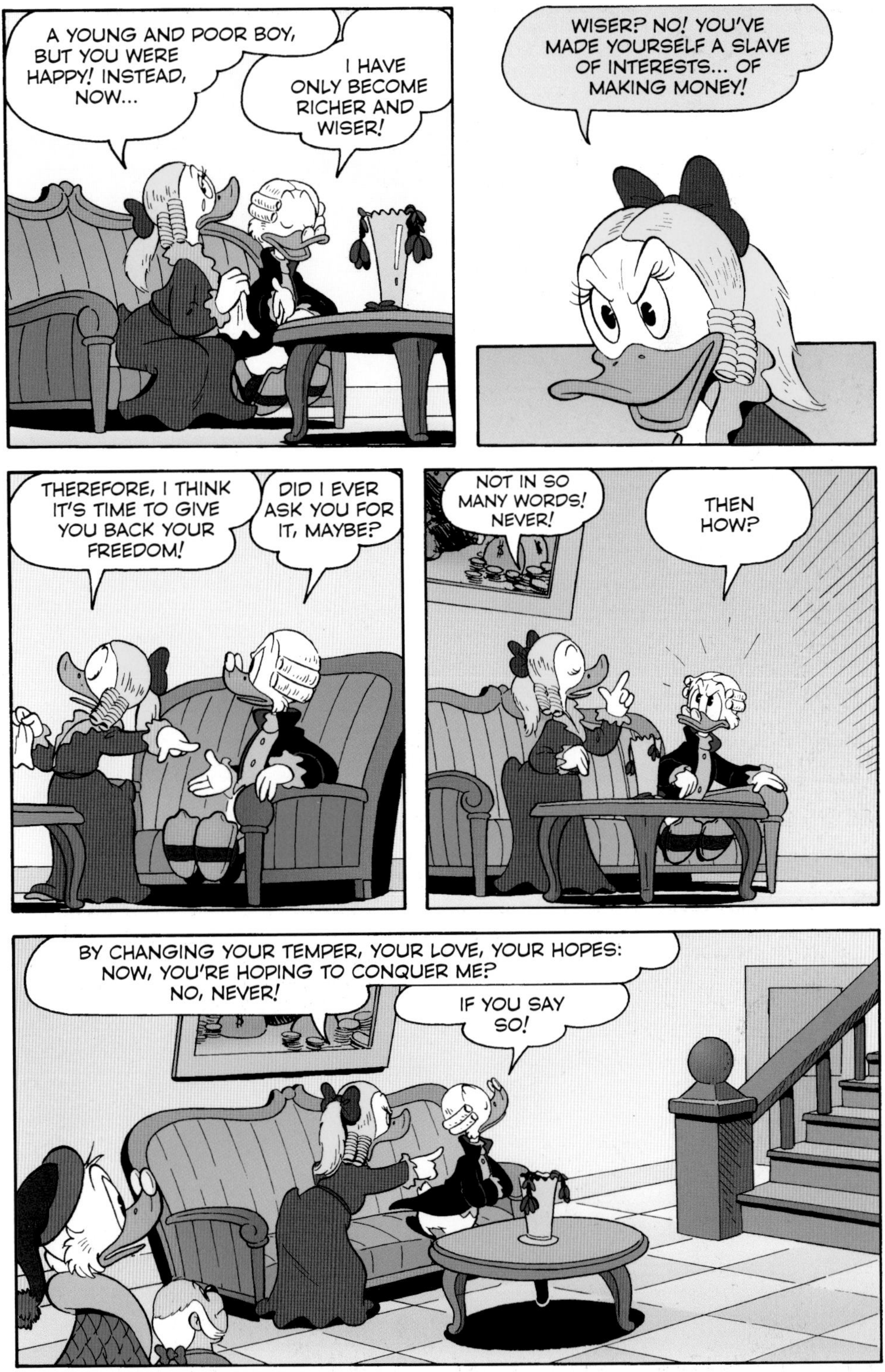
A YOUNG AND POOR BOY, BUT YOU WERE HAPPY! INSTEAD, NOW...
I HAVE ONLY BECOME RICHER AND WISER!
WISER? NO! YOU'VE MADE YOURSELF A SLAVE OF INTERESTS... OF MAKING MONEY!
THEREFORE, I THINK IT'S TIME TO GIVE YOU BACK YOUR FREEDOM!
DID I EVER ASK YOU FOR IT, MAYBE?
NOT IN SO MANY WORDS! NEVER!
THEN HOW?
BY CHANGING YOUR TEMPER, YOUR LOVE, YOUR HOPES: NOW, YOU'RE HOPING TO CONQUER ME? NO, NEVER!
IF YOU SAY SO!

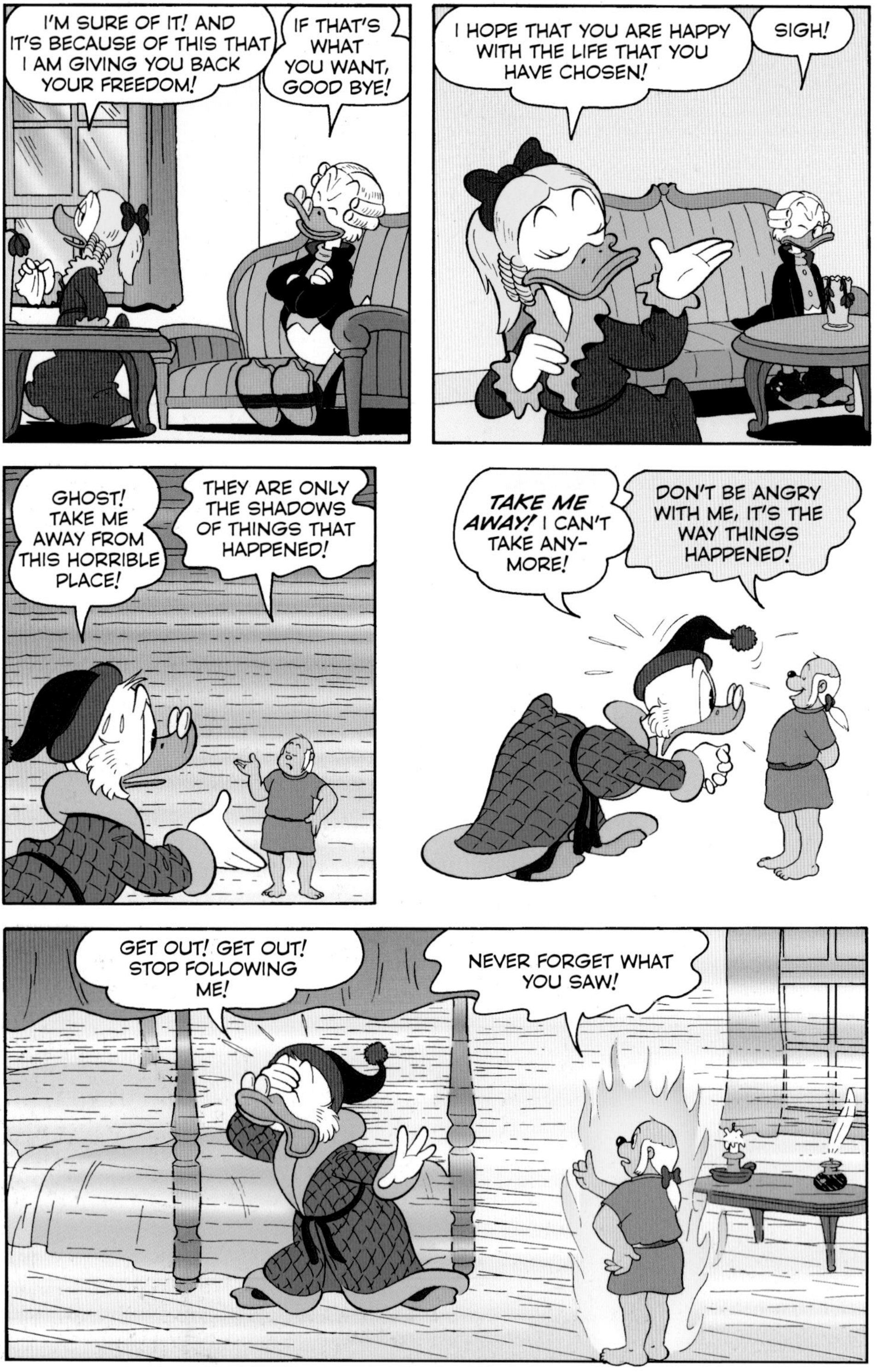
I'M SURE OF IT! AND IT'S BECAUSE OF THIS THAT I AM GIVING YOU BACK YOUR FREEDOM!
IF THAT'S WHAT YOU WANT, GOOD BYE!
I HOPE THAT YOU ARE HAPPY WITH THE LIFE THAT YOU HAVE CHOSEN!
SIGH!
GHOST! TAKE ME AWAY FROM THIS HORRIBLE PLACE!
THEY ARE ONLY THE SHADOWS OF THINGS THAT HAPPENED!
TAKE ME AWAY! I CAN'T TAKE ANY-MORE!
DON'T BE ANGRY WITH ME, IT'S THE WAY THINGS HAPPENED!
GET OUT! GET OUT! STOP FOLLOWING ME!
NEVER FORGET WHAT YOU SAW!

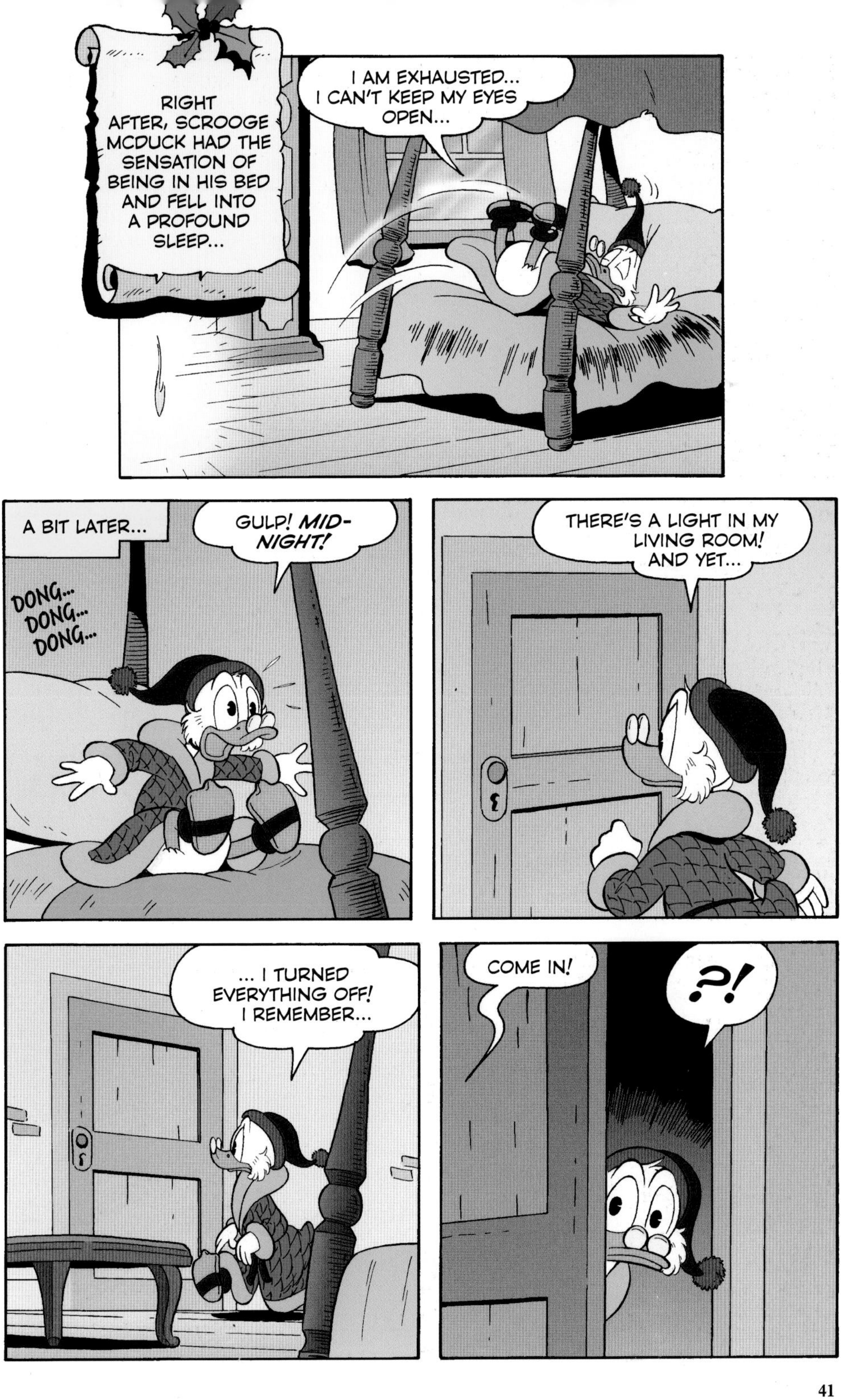
RIGHT AFTER, SCROOGE MCDUCK HAD THE SENSATION OF BEING IN HIS BED AND FELL INTO A PROFOUND SLEEP...
I AM EXHAUSTED... I CAN'T KEEP MY EYES OPEN...
A BIT LATER...
GULP! *MID-NIGHT!*
DONG... DONG... DONG...
THERE'S A LIGHT IN MY LIVING ROOM! AND YET...
... I TURNED EVERYTHING OFF! I REMEMBER...
COME IN!
?!

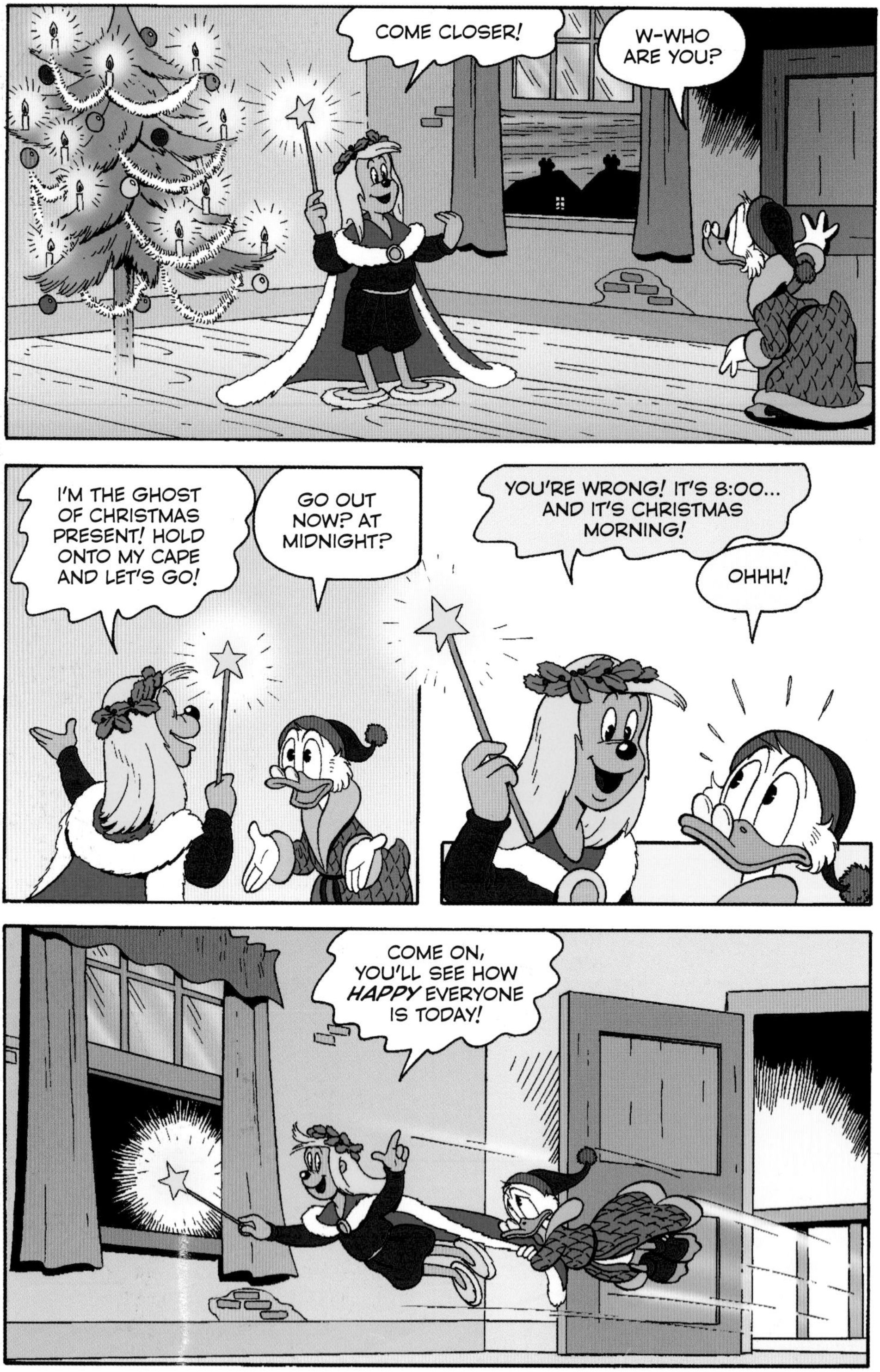
COME CLOSER!
W-WHO ARE YOU?
I'M THE GHOST OF CHRISTMAS PRESENT! HOLD ONTO MY CAPE AND LET'S GO!
GO OUT NOW? AT MIDNIGHT?
YOU'RE WRONG! IT'S 8:00... AND IT'S CHRISTMAS MORNING!
OHHH!
COME ON, YOU'LL SEE HOW *HAPPY* EVERYONE IS TODAY!

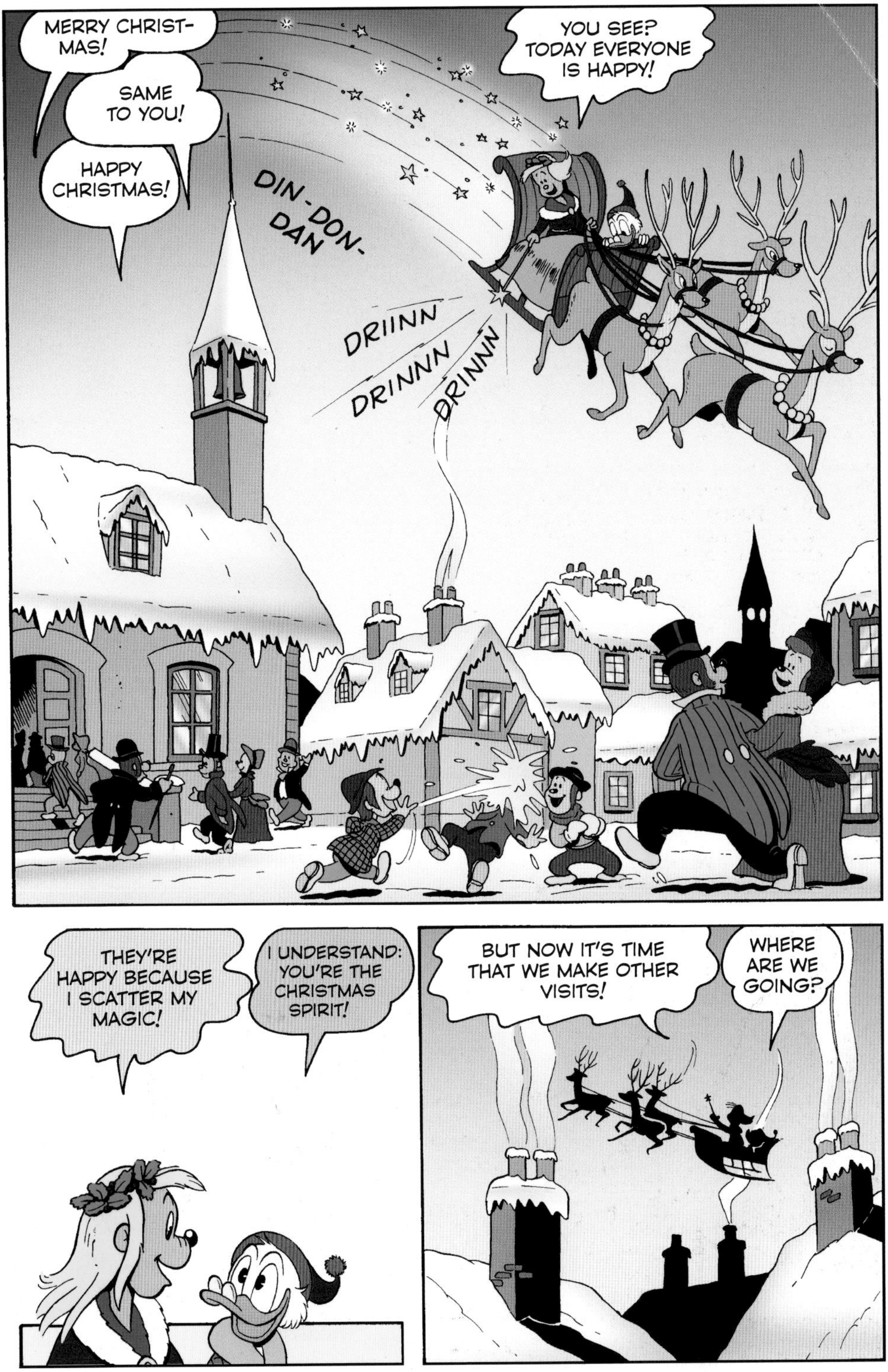
MERRY CHRIST-MAS!
SAME TO YOU!
HAPPY CHRISTMAS!
DIN-DON-DAN
YOU SEE? TODAY EVERYONE IS HAPPY!
DRIINN
DRINNN
DRINNN
THEY'RE HAPPY BECAUSE I SCATTER MY MAGIC!
I UNDERSTAND: YOU'RE THE CHRISTMAS SPIRIT!
BUT NOW IT'S TIME THAT WE MAKE OTHER VISITS!
WHERE ARE WE GOING?

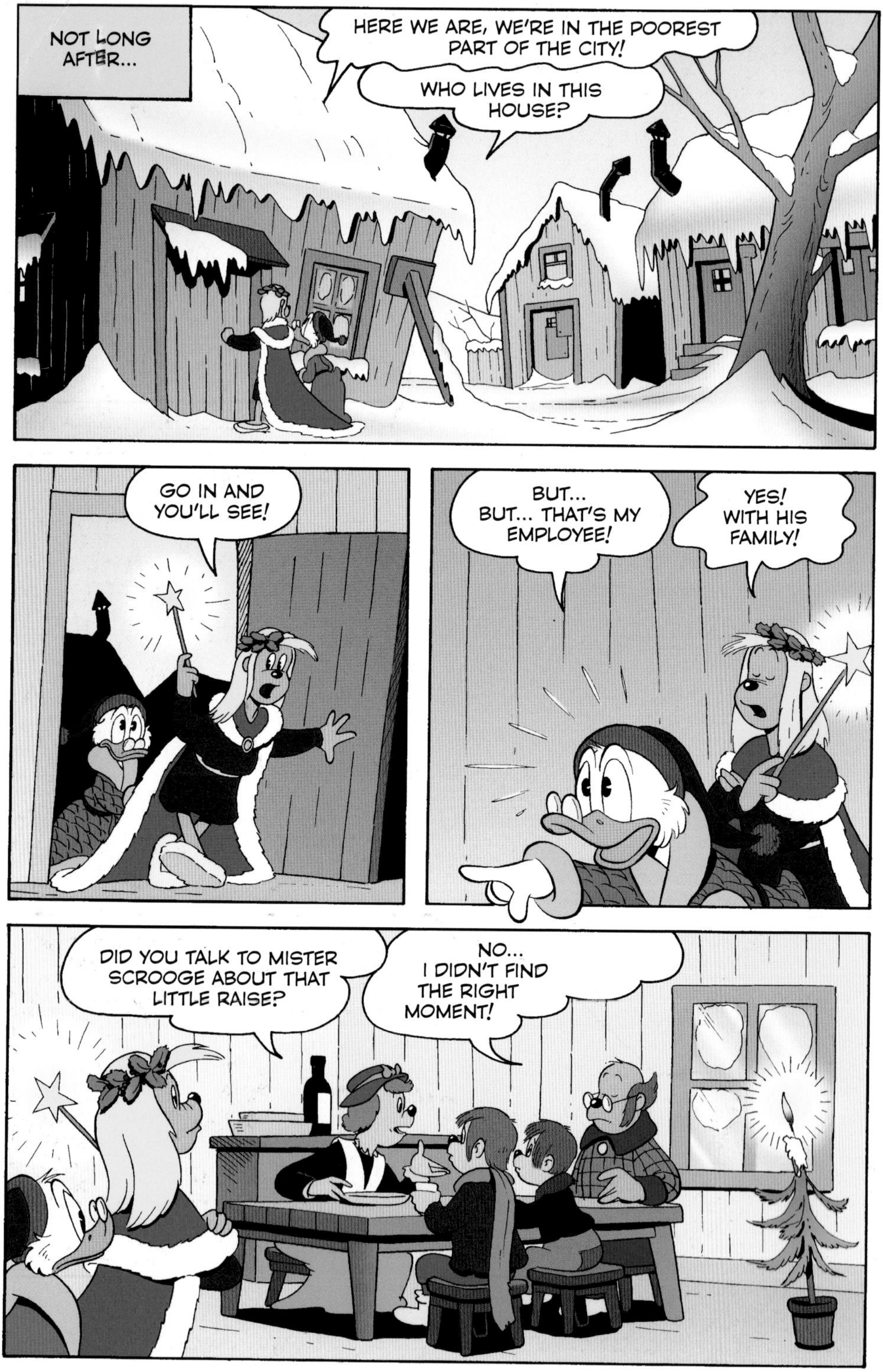
NOT LONG AFTER...
HERE WE ARE, WE'RE IN THE POOREST PART OF THE CITY!
WHO LIVES IN THIS HOUSE?
GO IN AND YOU'LL SEE!
BUT... BUT... THAT'S MY EMPLOYEE!
YES! WITH HIS FAMILY!
DID YOU TALK TO MISTER SCROOGE ABOUT THAT LITTLE RAISE?
NO... I DIDN'T FIND THE RIGHT MOMENT!

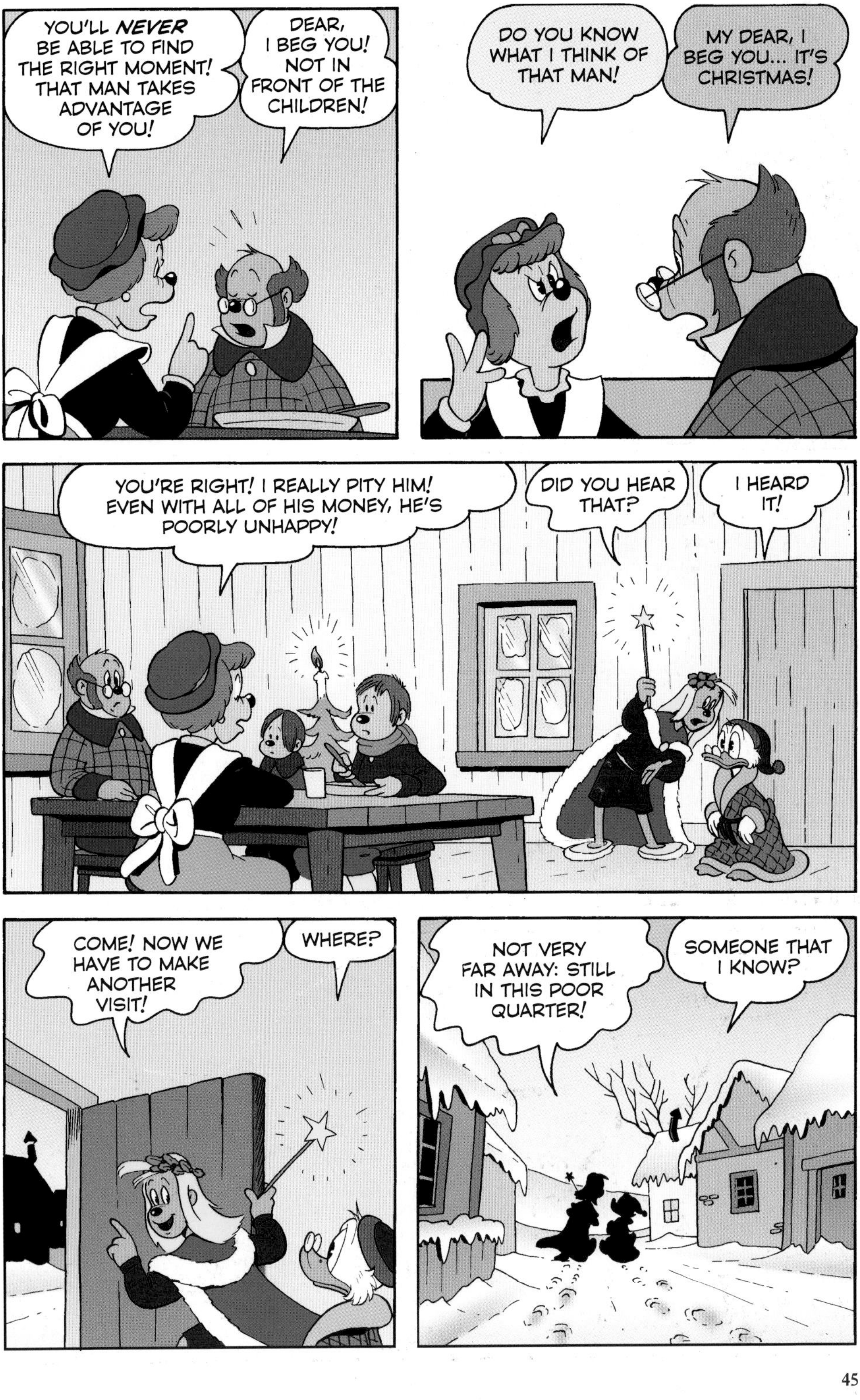
YOU'LL *NEVER* BE ABLE TO FIND THE RIGHT MOMENT! THAT MAN TAKES ADVANTAGE OF YOU!
DEAR, I BEG YOU! NOT IN FRONT OF THE CHILDREN!
DO YOU KNOW WHAT I THINK OF THAT MAN!
MY DEAR, I BEG YOU... IT'S CHRISTMAS!
YOU'RE RIGHT! I REALLY PITY HIM! EVEN WITH ALL OF HIS MONEY, HE'S POORLY UNHAPPY!
DID YOU HEAR THAT?
I HEARD IT!
COME! NOW WE HAVE TO MAKE ANOTHER VISIT!
WHERE?
NOT VERY FAR AWAY: STILL IN THIS POOR QUARTER!
SOMEONE THAT I KNOW?

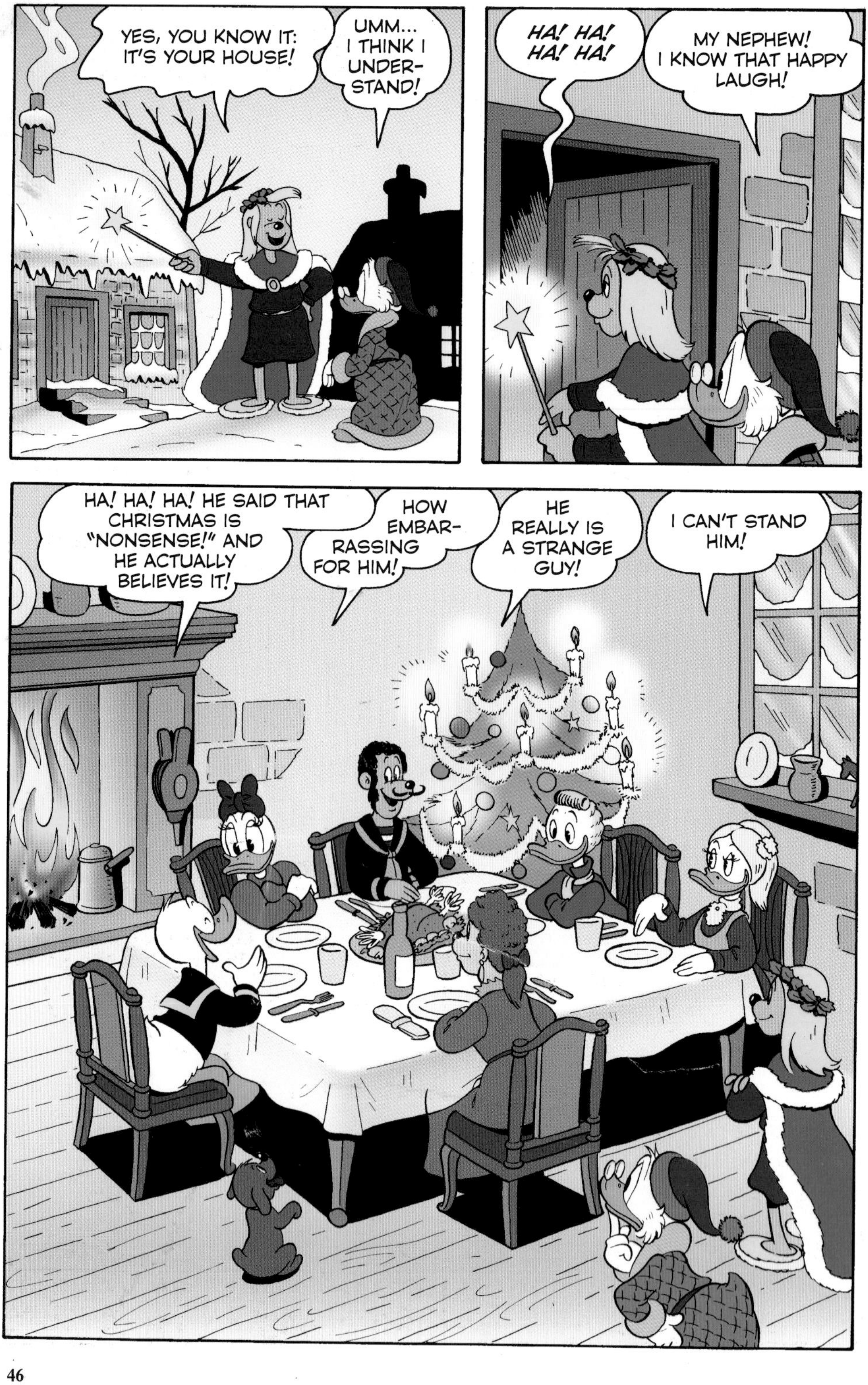
YES, YOU KNOW IT: IT'S YOUR HOUSE!
UMM... I THINK I UNDER-STAND!
HA! HA! HA! HA!
MY NEPHEW! I KNOW THAT HAPPY LAUGH!
HA! HA! HA! HE SAID THAT CHRISTMAS IS "NONSENSE!" AND HE ACTUALLY BELIEVES IT!
HOW EMBAR-RASSING FOR HIM!
HE REALLY IS A STRANGE GUY!
I CAN'T STAND HIM!

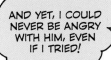

AND YET, I COULD NEVER BE ANGRY WITH HIM, EVEN IF I TRIED!

YOU'RE TOO GOOD, MY HUSBAND! *TOO* GOOD!

HE HAS NO FEELING TOWARDS YOU! HE EVEN REFUSED YOUR INVITATION TO LUNCH!

OH! HE DIDN'T REALLY MISS A BIG LUNCH!

HUMPF! YOU ARE REALLY MEAN!

ON THE CONTRARY: IT WAS AN EXQUISITE LUNCH!

YOU SHOULD BE EMBAR-RASSED FOR TALKING THAT WAY!

ALL RIGHT! ALL RIGHT! I ADMIT THAT I WAS JOKING!

DO YOU FORGIVE ME, MY DEAR?

YOU DON'T DESERVE IT! BUT... SINCE IT'S CHRISTMAS...

MERRY CHRISTMAS TO OLD UNCLE SCROOGE! HE WOULDN'T ACCEPT GOOD WISHES FROM ME, BUT I WILL SEND THEM TO HIM ANYWAY!

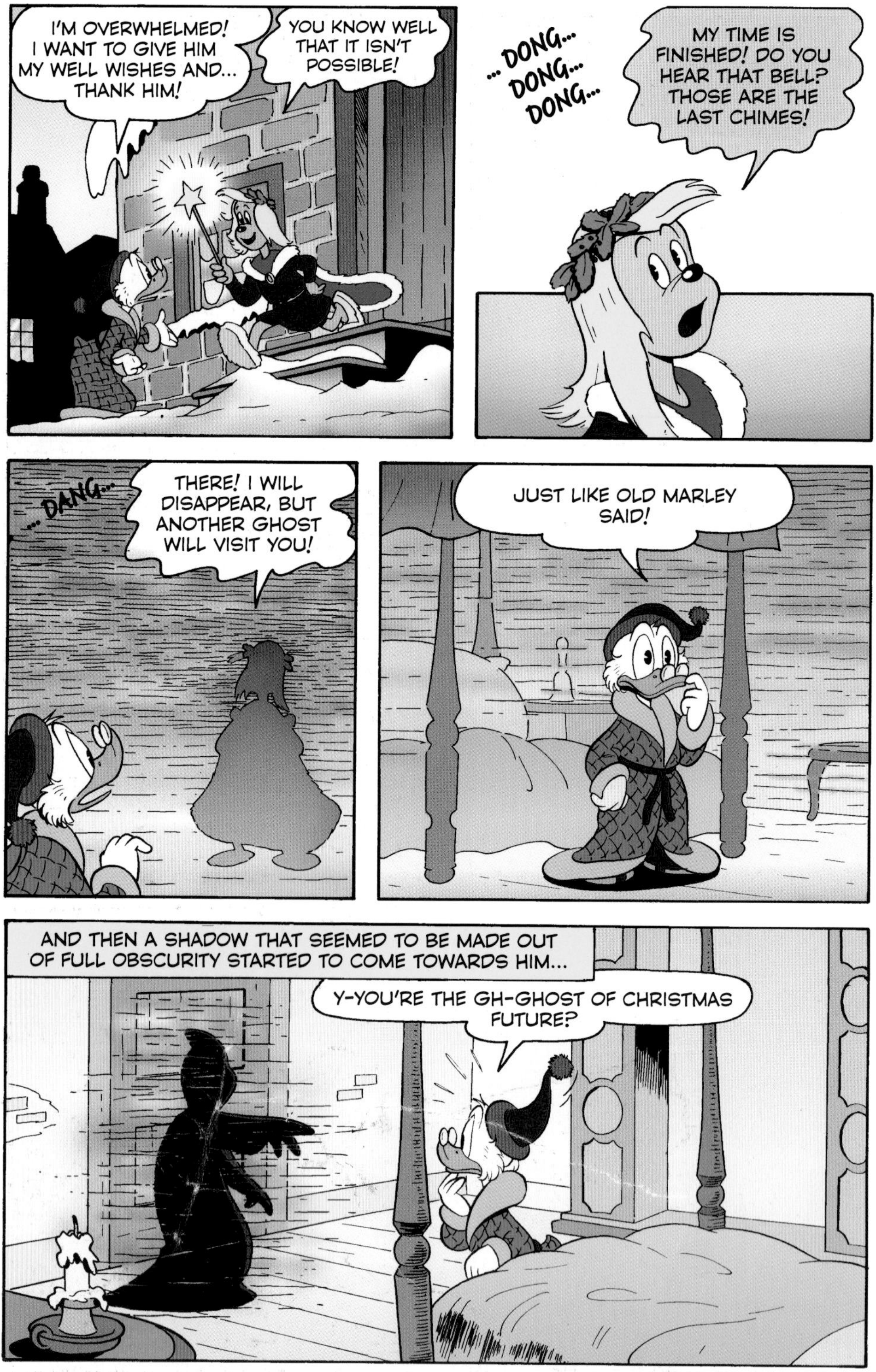

I'M OVERWHELMED! I WANT TO GIVE HIM MY WELL WISHES AND... THANK HIM!
YOU KNOW WELL THAT IT ISN'T POSSIBLE!
... DONG... DONG... DONG...
MY TIME IS FINISHED! DO YOU HEAR THAT BELL? THOSE ARE THE LAST CHIMES!
... DANG...
THERE! I WILL DISAPPEAR, BUT ANOTHER GHOST WILL VISIT YOU!
JUST LIKE OLD MARLEY SAID!
AND THEN A SHADOW THAT SEEMED TO BE MADE OUT OF FULL OBSCURITY STARTED TO COME TOWARDS HIM...
Y-YOU'RE THE GH-GHOST OF CHRISTMAS FUTURE?

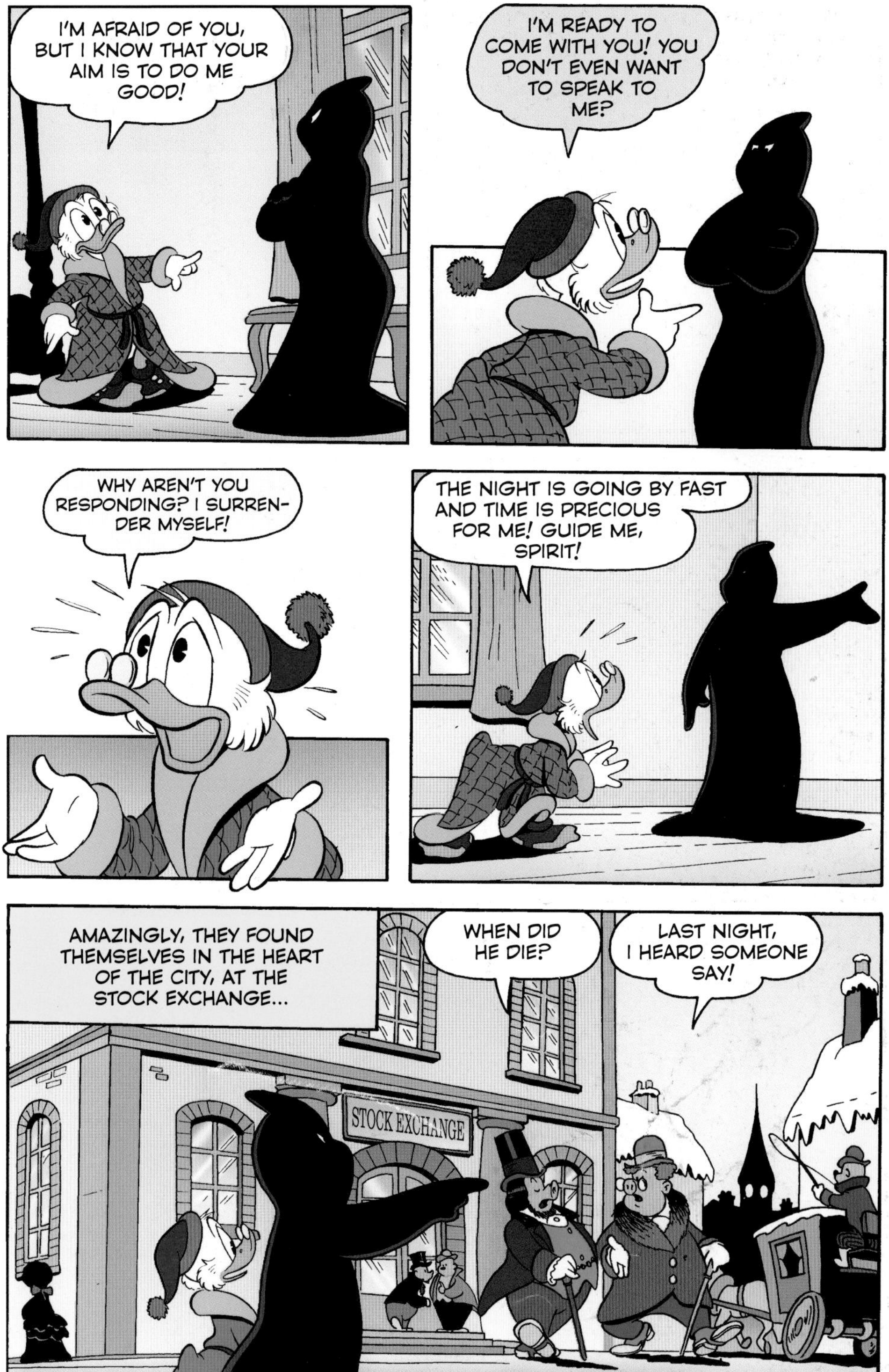
I'M AFRAID OF YOU, BUT I KNOW THAT YOUR AIM IS TO DO ME GOOD!
I'M READY TO COME WITH YOU! YOU DON'T EVEN WANT TO SPEAK TO ME?
WHY AREN'T YOU RESPONDING? I SURREN-DER MYSELF!
THE NIGHT IS GOING BY FAST AND TIME IS PRECIOUS FOR ME! GUIDE ME, SPIRIT!
AMAZINGLY, THEY FOUND THEMSELVES IN THE HEART OF THE CITY, AT THE STOCK EXCHANGE...
WHEN DID HE DIE?
LAST NIGHT, I HEARD SOMEONE SAY!
STOCK EXCHANGE

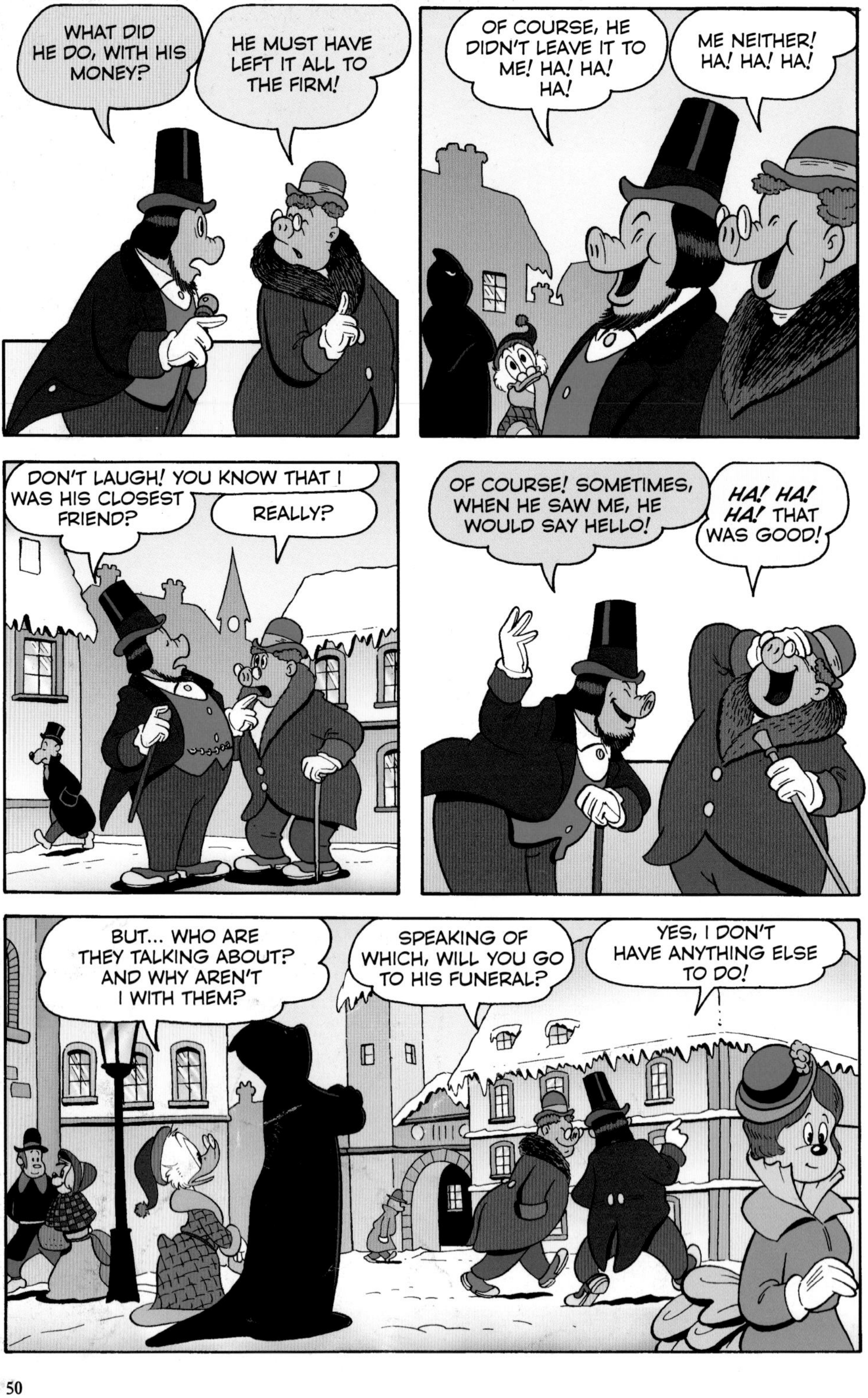
WHAT DID HE DO, WITH HIS MONEY?
HE MUST HAVE LEFT IT ALL TO THE FIRM!
OF COURSE, HE DIDN'T LEAVE IT TO ME! HA! HA! HA!
ME NEITHER! HA! HA! HA!
DON'T LAUGH! YOU KNOW THAT I WAS HIS CLOSEST FRIEND?
REALLY?
OF COURSE! SOMETIMES, WHEN HE SAW ME, HE WOULD SAY HELLO!
HA! HA! HA! THAT WAS GOOD!
BUT... WHO ARE THEY TALKING ABOUT? AND WHY AREN'T I WITH THEM?
SPEAKING OF WHICH, WILL YOU GO TO HIS FUNERAL?
YES, I DON'T HAVE ANYTHING ELSE TO DO!

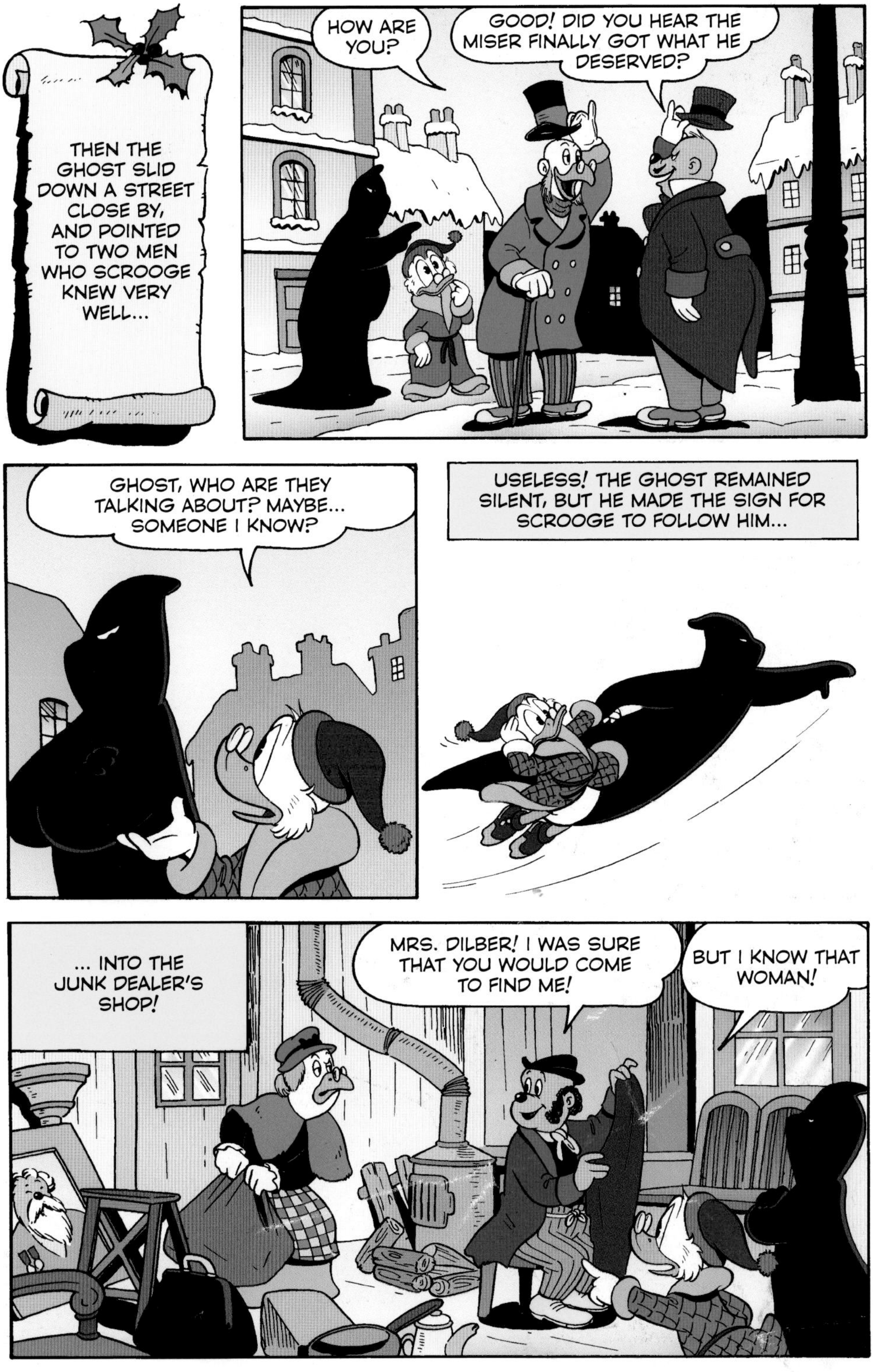
THEN THE GHOST SLID DOWN A STREET CLOSE BY, AND POINTED TO TWO MEN WHO SCROOGE KNEW VERY WELL...
HOW ARE YOU?
GOOD! DID YOU HEAR THE MISER FINALLY GOT WHAT HE DESERVED?
GHOST, WHO ARE THEY TALKING ABOUT? MAYBE... SOMEONE I KNOW?
USELESS! THE GHOST REMAINED SILENT, BUT HE MADE THE SIGN FOR SCROOGE TO FOLLOW HIM...
... INTO THE JUNK DEALER'S SHOP!
MRS. DILBER! I WAS SURE THAT YOU WOULD COME TO FIND ME!
BUT I KNOW THAT WOMAN!

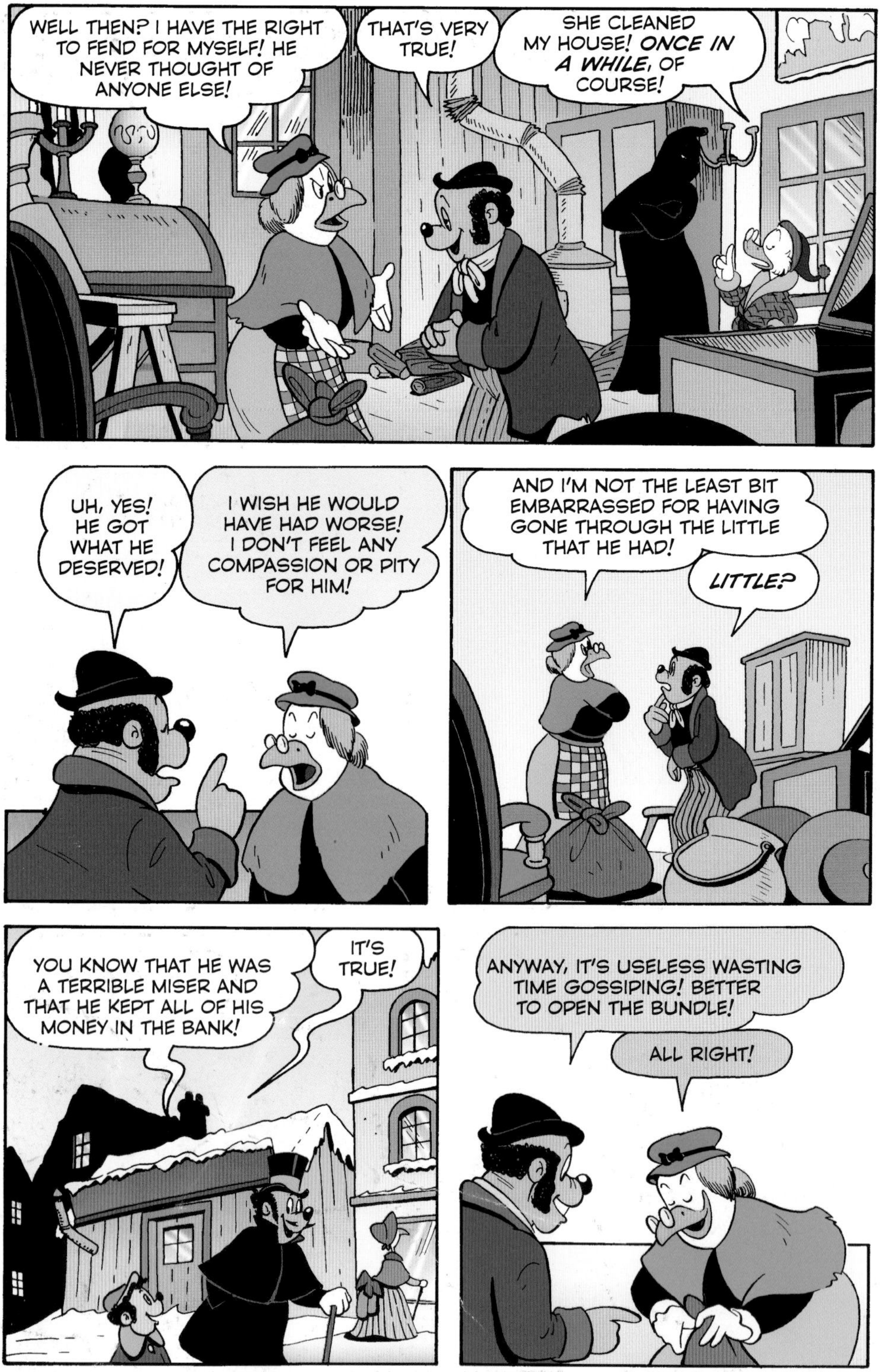
WELL THEN? I HAVE THE RIGHT TO FEND FOR MYSELF! HE NEVER THOUGHT OF ANYONE ELSE!
THAT'S VERY TRUE!
SHE CLEANED MY HOUSE! ONCE IN A WHILE, OF COURSE!
UH, YES! HE GOT WHAT HE DESERVED!
I WISH HE WOULD HAVE HAD WORSE! I DON'T FEEL ANY COMPASSION OR PITY FOR HIM!
AND I'M NOT THE LEAST BIT EMBARRASSED FOR HAVING GONE THROUGH THE LITTLE THAT HE HAD!
LITTLE?
YOU KNOW THAT HE WAS A TERRIBLE MISER AND THAT HE KEPT ALL OF HIS MONEY IN THE BANK!
IT'S TRUE!
ANYWAY, IT'S USELESS WASTING TIME GOSSIPING! BETTER TO OPEN THE BUNDLE!
ALL RIGHT!

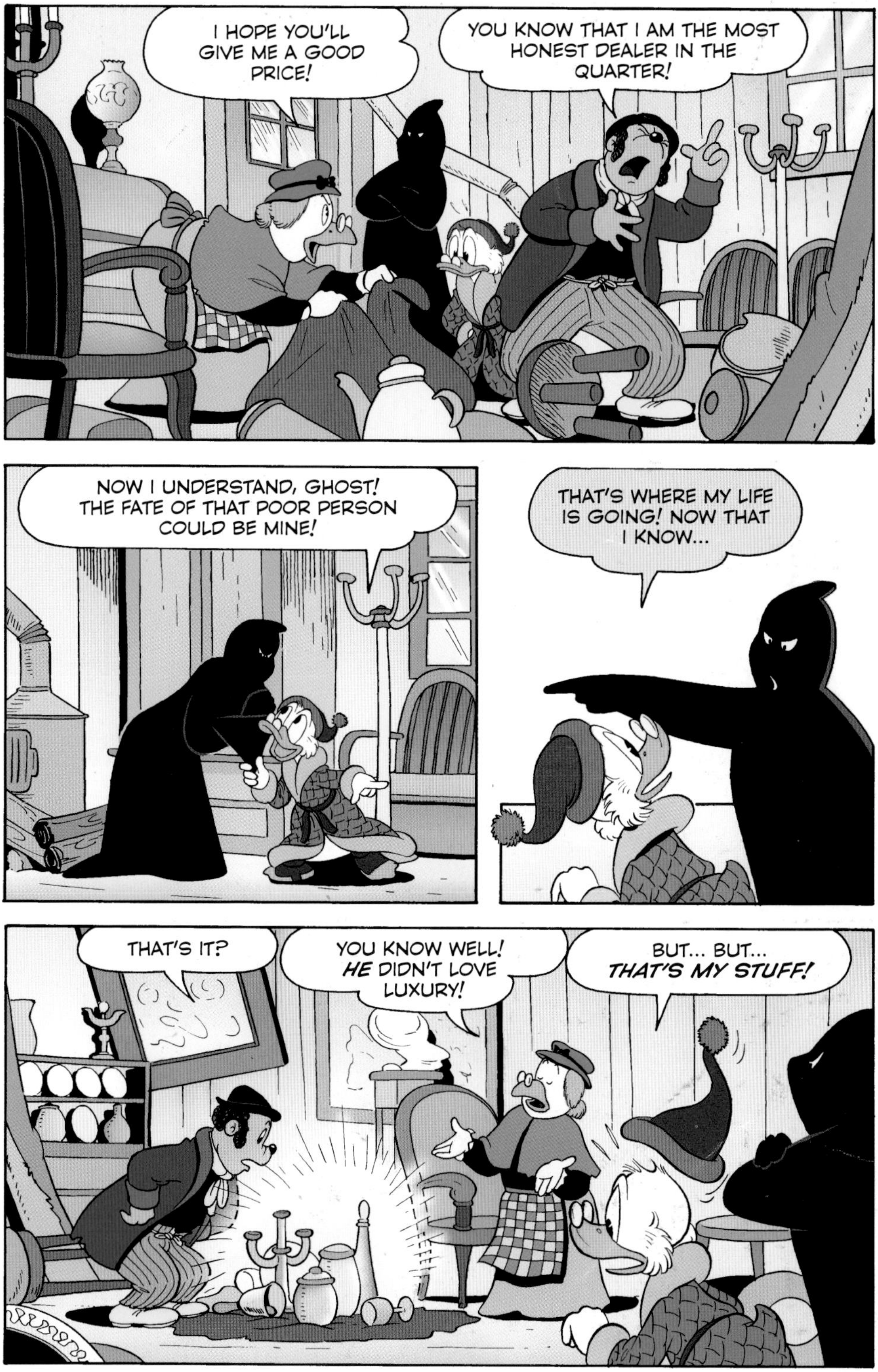
I HOPE YOU'LL GIVE ME A GOOD PRICE!
YOU KNOW THAT I AM THE MOST HONEST DEALER IN THE QUARTER!
NOW I UNDERSTAND, GHOST! THE FATE OF THAT POOR PERSON COULD BE MINE!
THAT'S WHERE MY LIFE IS GOING! NOW THAT I KNOW...
THAT'S IT?
YOU KNOW WELL! *HE* DIDN'T LOVE LUXURY!
BUT... BUT... *THAT'S MY STUFF!*

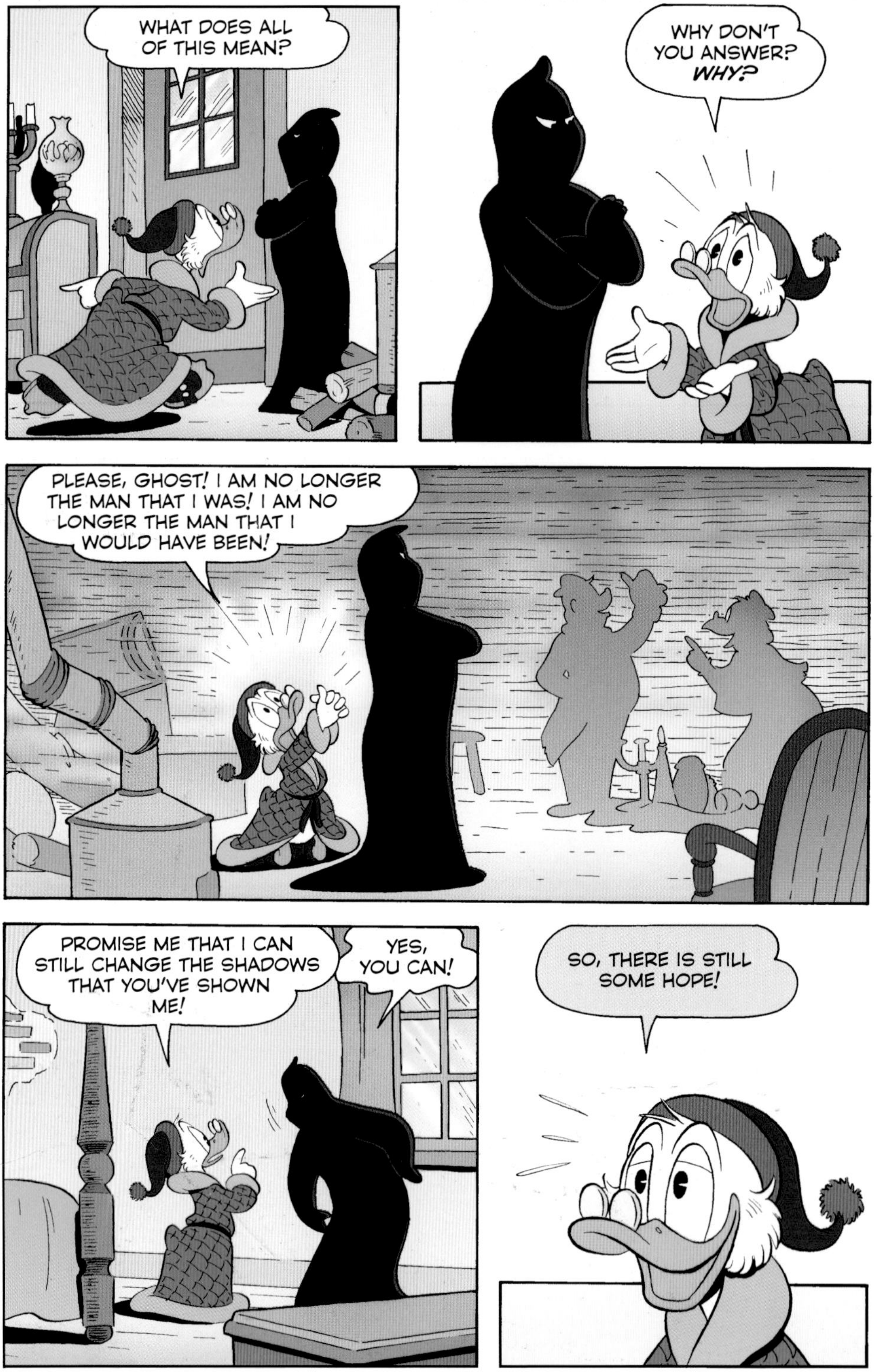
WHAT DOES ALL OF THIS MEAN?
WHY DON'T YOU ANSWER? *WHY?*
PLEASE, GHOST! I AM NO LONGER THE MAN THAT I WAS! I AM NO LONGER THE MAN THAT I WOULD HAVE BEEN!
PROMISE ME THAT I CAN STILL CHANGE THE SHADOWS THAT YOU'VE SHOWN ME!
YES, YOU CAN!
SO, THERE IS STILL SOME HOPE!

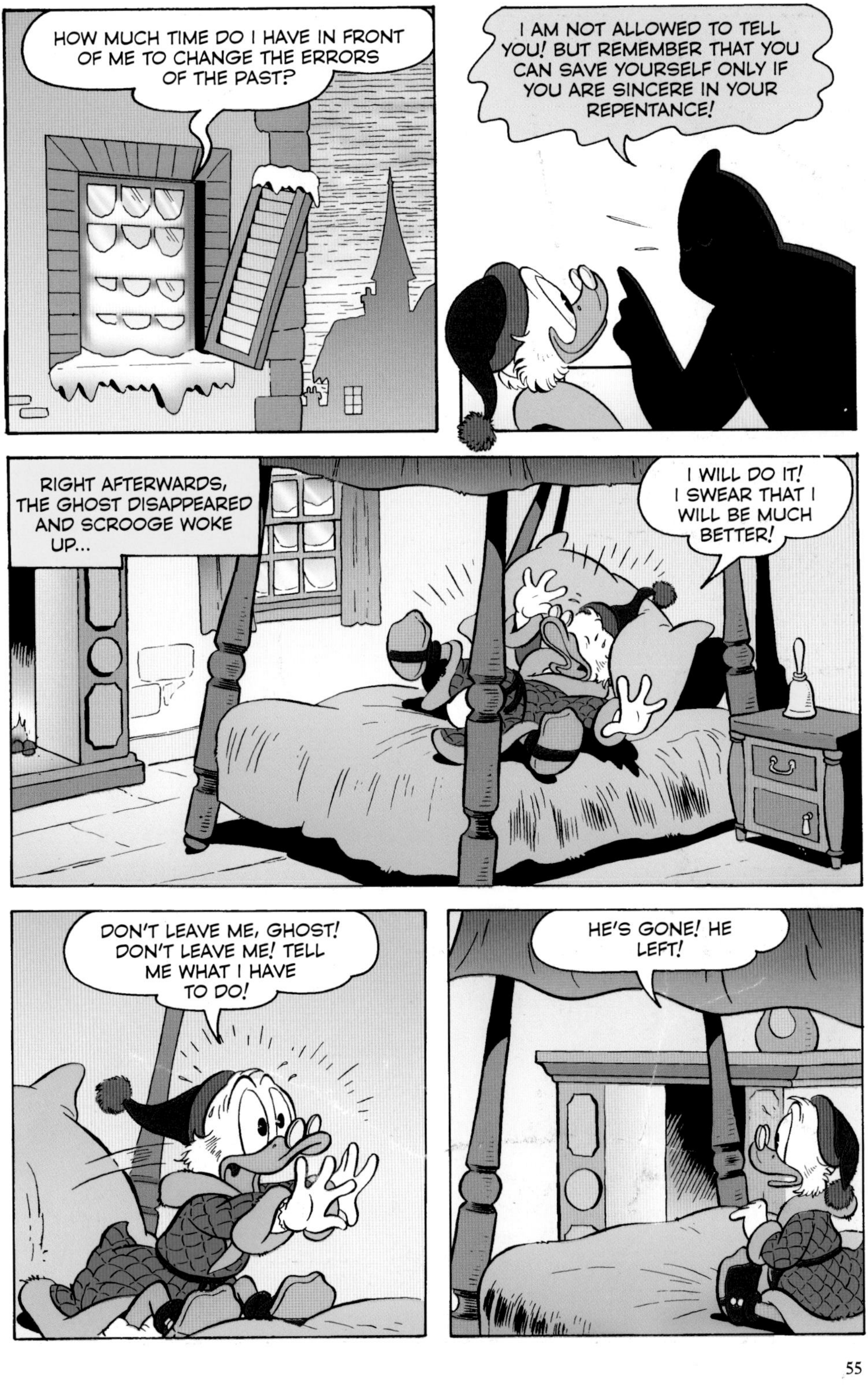
HOW MUCH TIME DO I HAVE IN FRONT OF ME TO CHANGE THE ERRORS OF THE PAST?
I AM NOT ALLOWED TO TELL YOU! BUT REMEMBER THAT YOU CAN SAVE YOURSELF ONLY IF YOU ARE SINCERE IN YOUR REPENTANCE!
RIGHT AFTERWARDS, THE GHOST DISAPPEARED AND SCROOGE WOKE UP...
I WILL DO IT! I SWEAR THAT I WILL BE MUCH BETTER!
DON'T LEAVE ME, GHOST! DON'T LEAVE ME! TELL ME WHAT I HAVE TO DO!
HE'S GONE! HE LEFT!

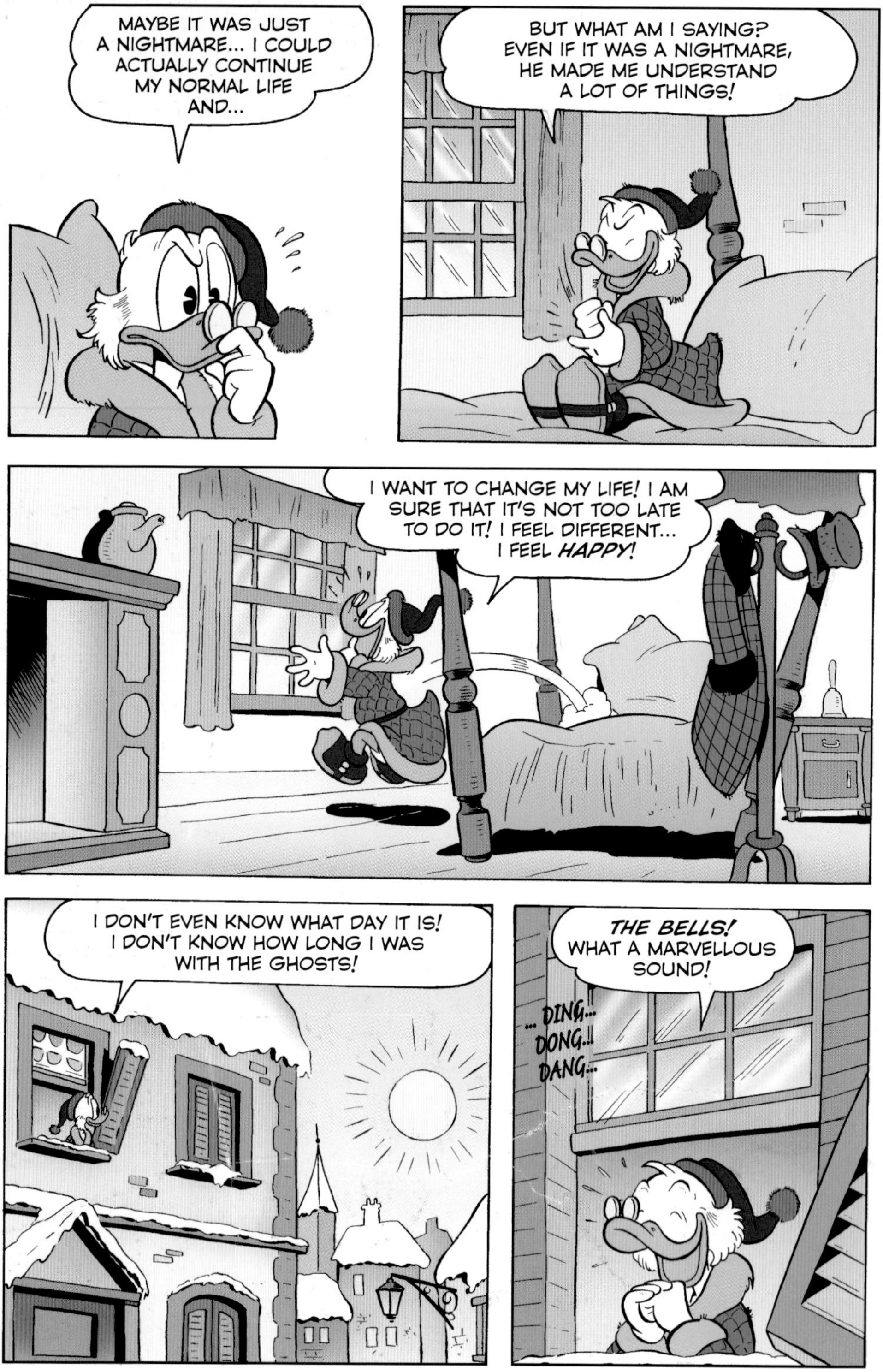
MAYBE IT WAS JUST A NIGHTMARE... I COULD ACTUALLY CONTINUE MY NORMAL LIFE AND...
BUT WHAT AM I SAYING? EVEN IF IT WAS A NIGHTMARE, HE MADE ME UNDERSTAND A LOT OF THINGS!
I WANT TO CHANGE MY LIFE! I AM SURE THAT IT'S NOT TOO LATE TO DO IT! I FEEL DIFFERENT... I FEEL HAPPY!
I DON'T EVEN KNOW WHAT DAY IT IS! I DON'T KNOW HOW LONG I WAS WITH THE GHOSTS!
THE BELLS! WHAT A MARVELLOUS SOUND!
... DING... DONG... DANG...

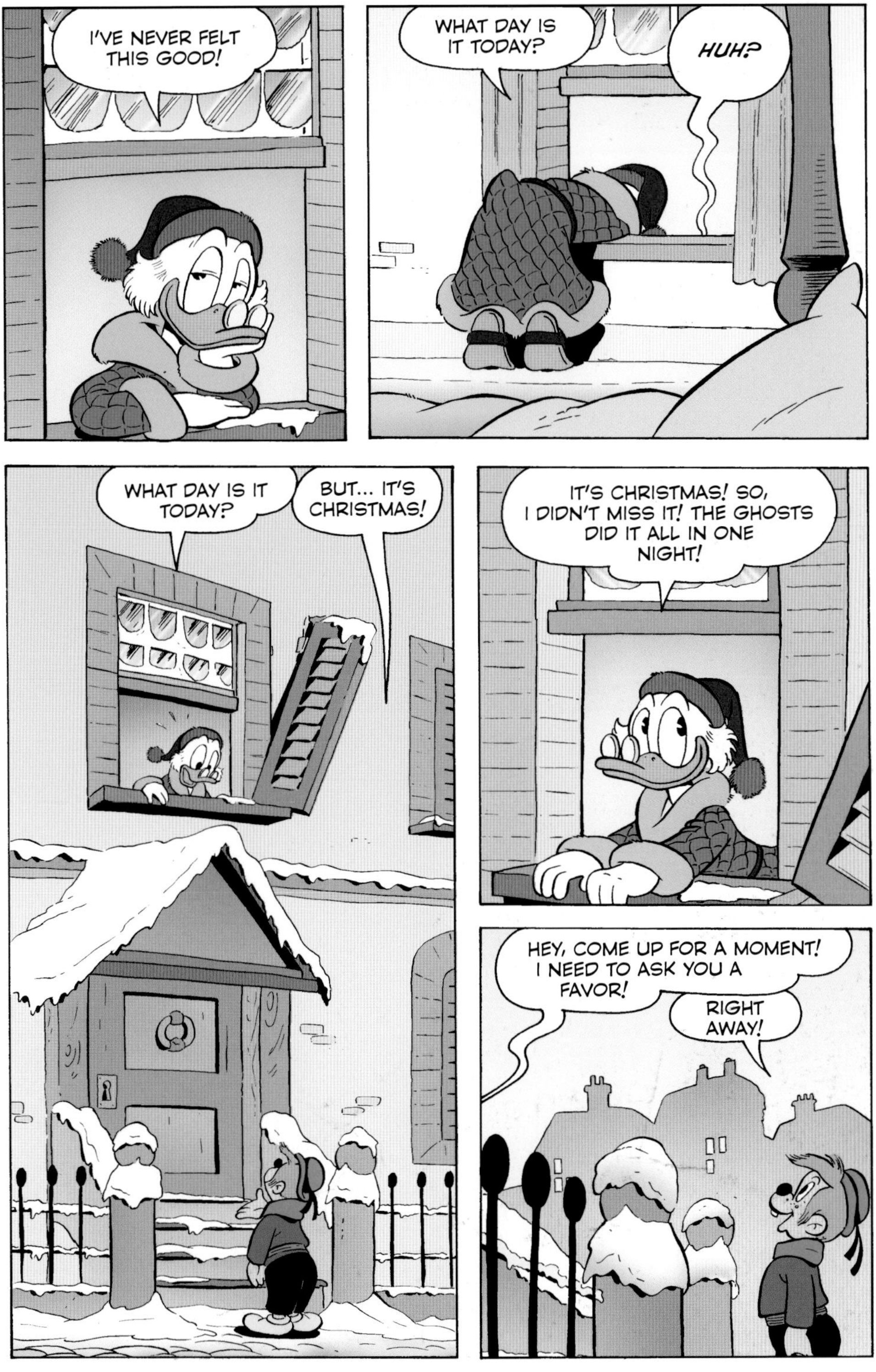
I'VE NEVER FELT THIS GOOD!
WHAT DAY IS IT TODAY?
HUH?
WHAT DAY IS IT TODAY?
BUT... IT'S CHRISTMAS!
IT'S CHRISTMAS! SO, I DIDN'T MISS IT! THE GHOSTS DID IT ALL IN ONE NIGHT!
HEY, COME UP FOR A MOMENT! I NEED TO ASK YOU A FAVOR!
RIGHT AWAY!

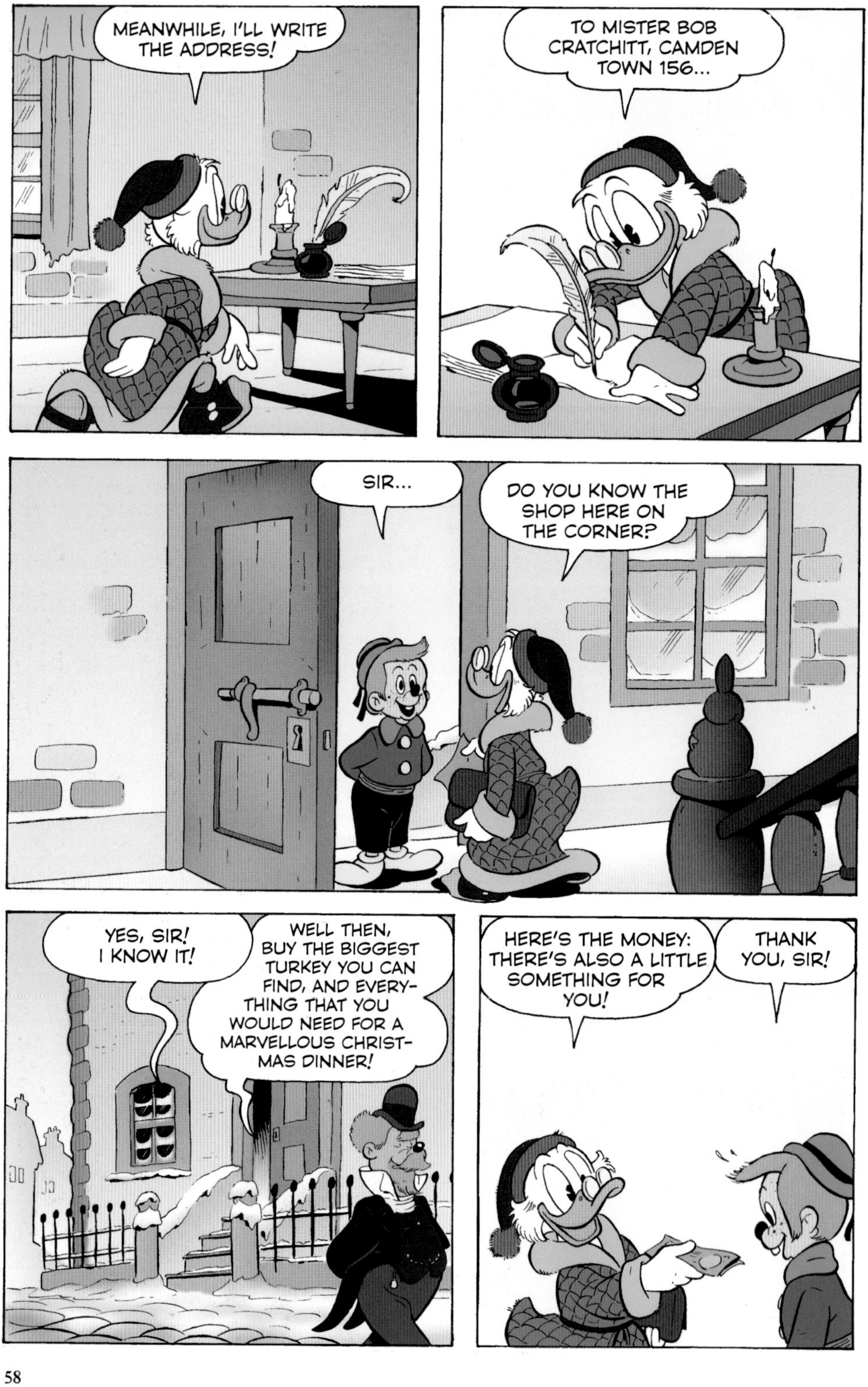
MEANWHILE, I'LL WRITE THE ADDRESS!
TO MISTER BOB CRATCHITT, CAMDEN TOWN 156...
SIR...
DO YOU KNOW THE SHOP HERE ON THE CORNER?
YES, SIR! I KNOW IT!
WELL THEN, BUY THE BIGGEST TURKEY YOU CAN FIND, AND EVERY-THING THAT YOU WOULD NEED FOR A MARVELLOUS CHRIST-MAS DINNER!
HERE'S THE MONEY: THERE'S ALSO A LITTLE SOMETHING FOR YOU!
THANK YOU, SIR!

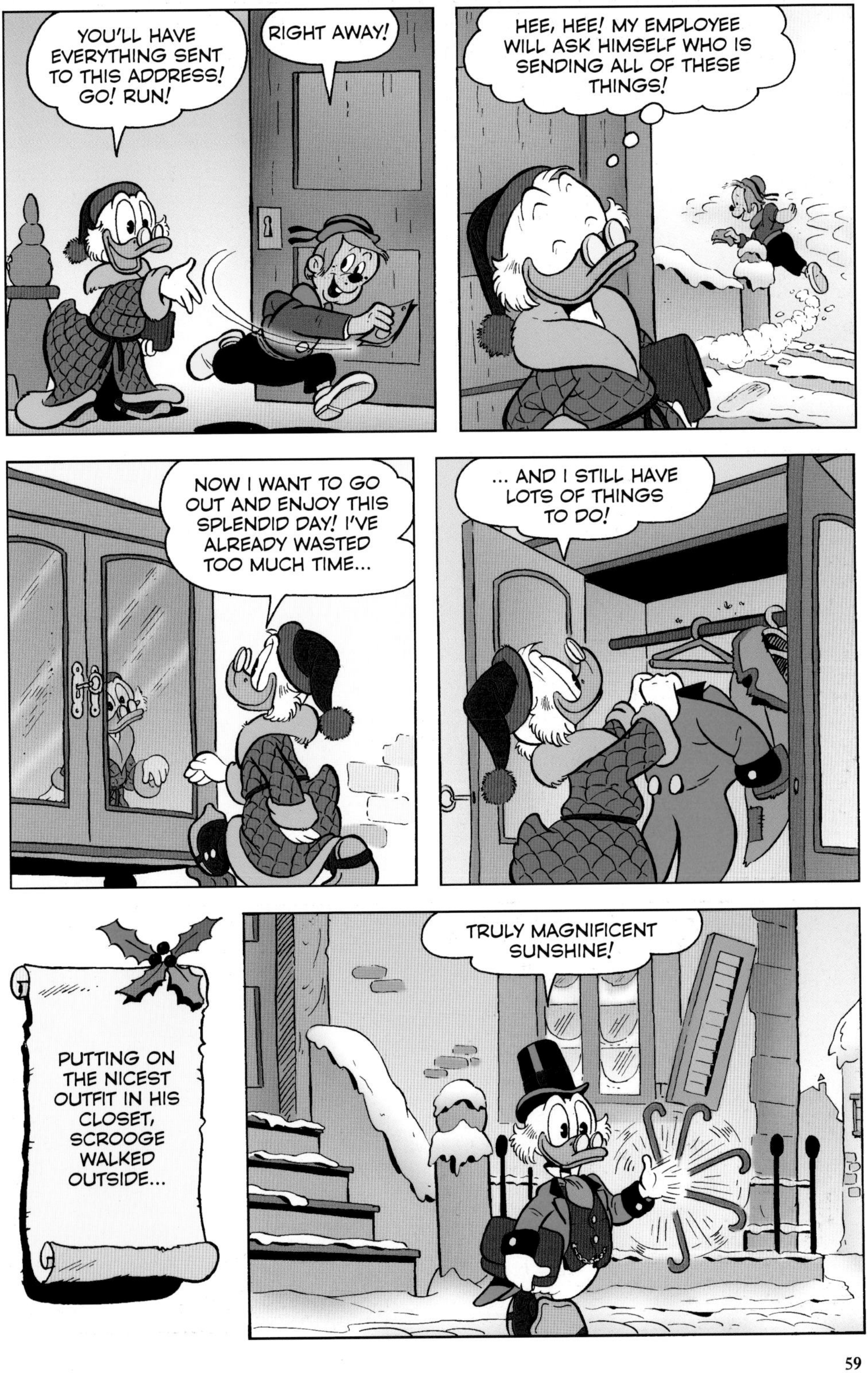
YOU'LL HAVE EVERYTHING SENT TO THIS ADDRESS! GO! RUN!
RIGHT AWAY!
HEE, HEE! MY EMPLOYEE WILL ASK HIMSELF WHO IS SENDING ALL OF THESE THINGS!
NOW I WANT TO GO OUT AND ENJOY THIS SPLENDID DAY! I'VE ALREADY WASTED TOO MUCH TIME...
... AND I STILL HAVE LOTS OF THINGS TO DO!
PUTTING ON THE NICEST OUTFIT IN HIS CLOSET, SCROOGE WALKED OUTSIDE...
TRULY MAGNIFICENT SUNSHINE!

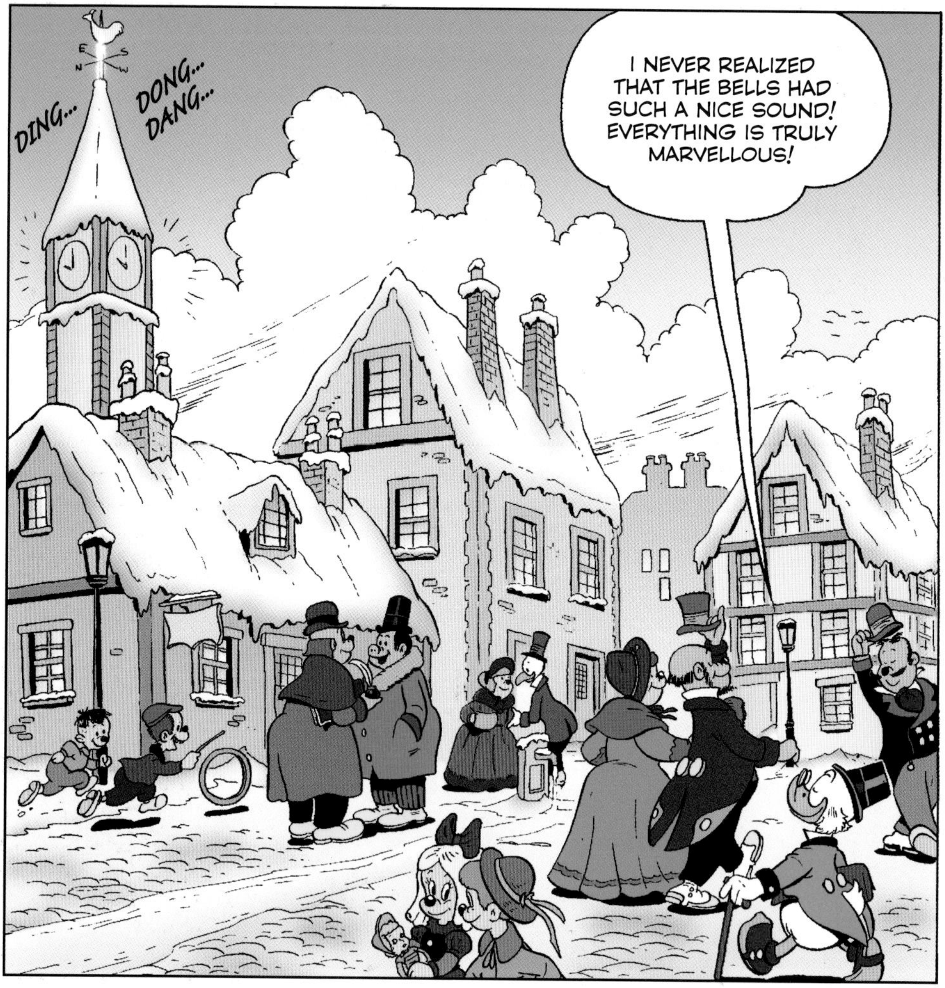
DING...
DONG... DANG...
I NEVER REALIZED THAT THE BELLS HAD SUCH A NICE SOUND! EVERYTHING IS TRULY MARVELLOUS!
E S N W

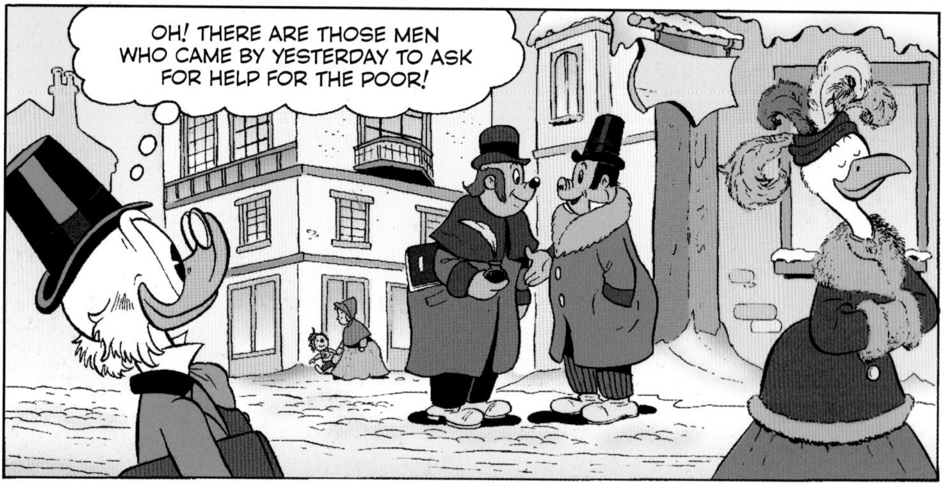
OH! THERE ARE THOSE MEN WHO CAME BY YESTERDAY TO ASK FOR HELP FOR THE POOR!

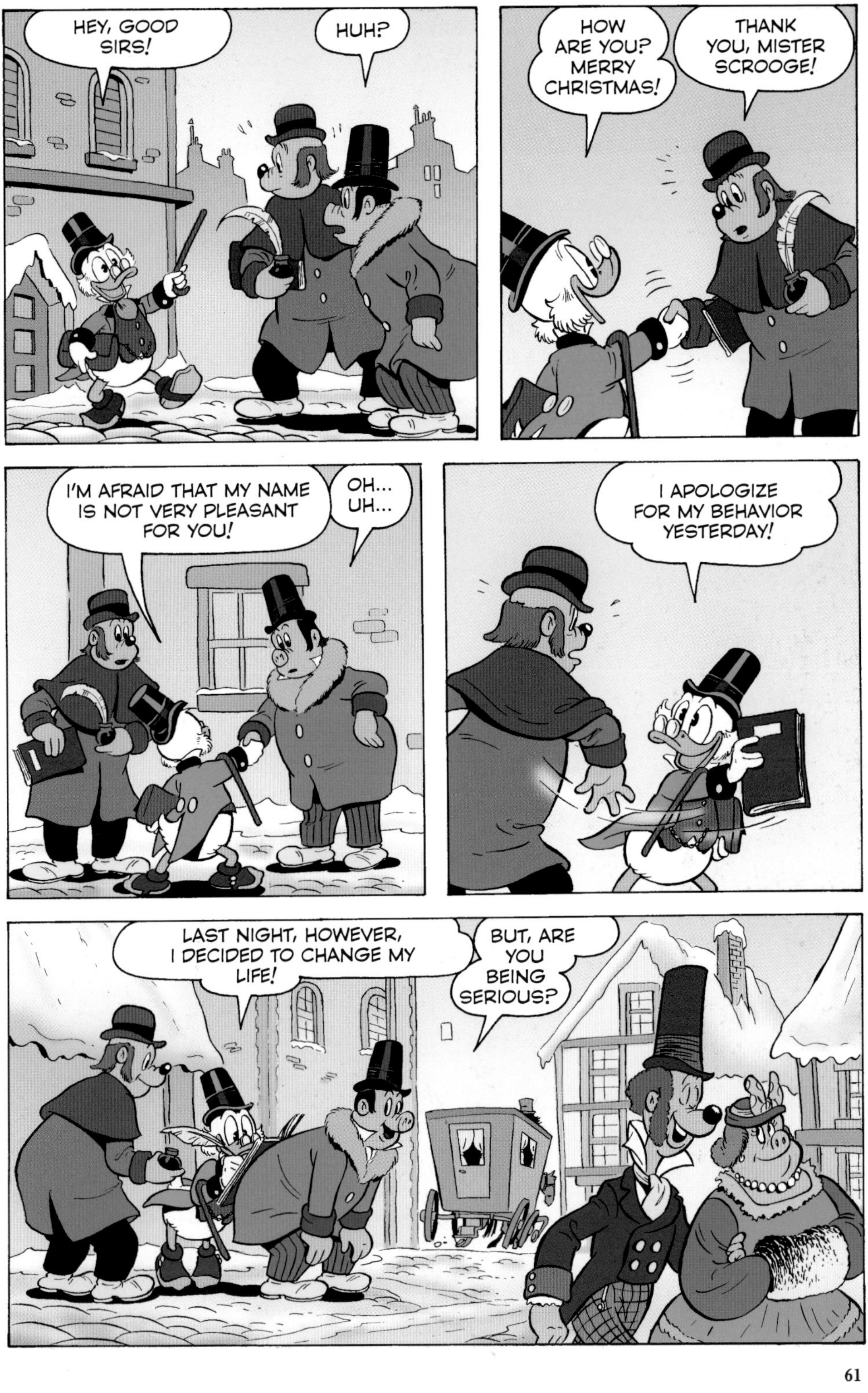
HEY, GOOD SIRS!
HUH?
HOW ARE YOU? MERRY CHRISTMAS!
THANK YOU, MISTER SCROOGE!
I'M AFRAID THAT MY NAME IS NOT VERY PLEASANT FOR YOU!
OH... UH...
I APOLOGIZE FOR MY BEHAVIOR YESTERDAY!
LAST NIGHT, HOWEVER, I DECIDED TO CHANGE MY LIFE!
BUT, ARE YOU BEING SERIOUS?

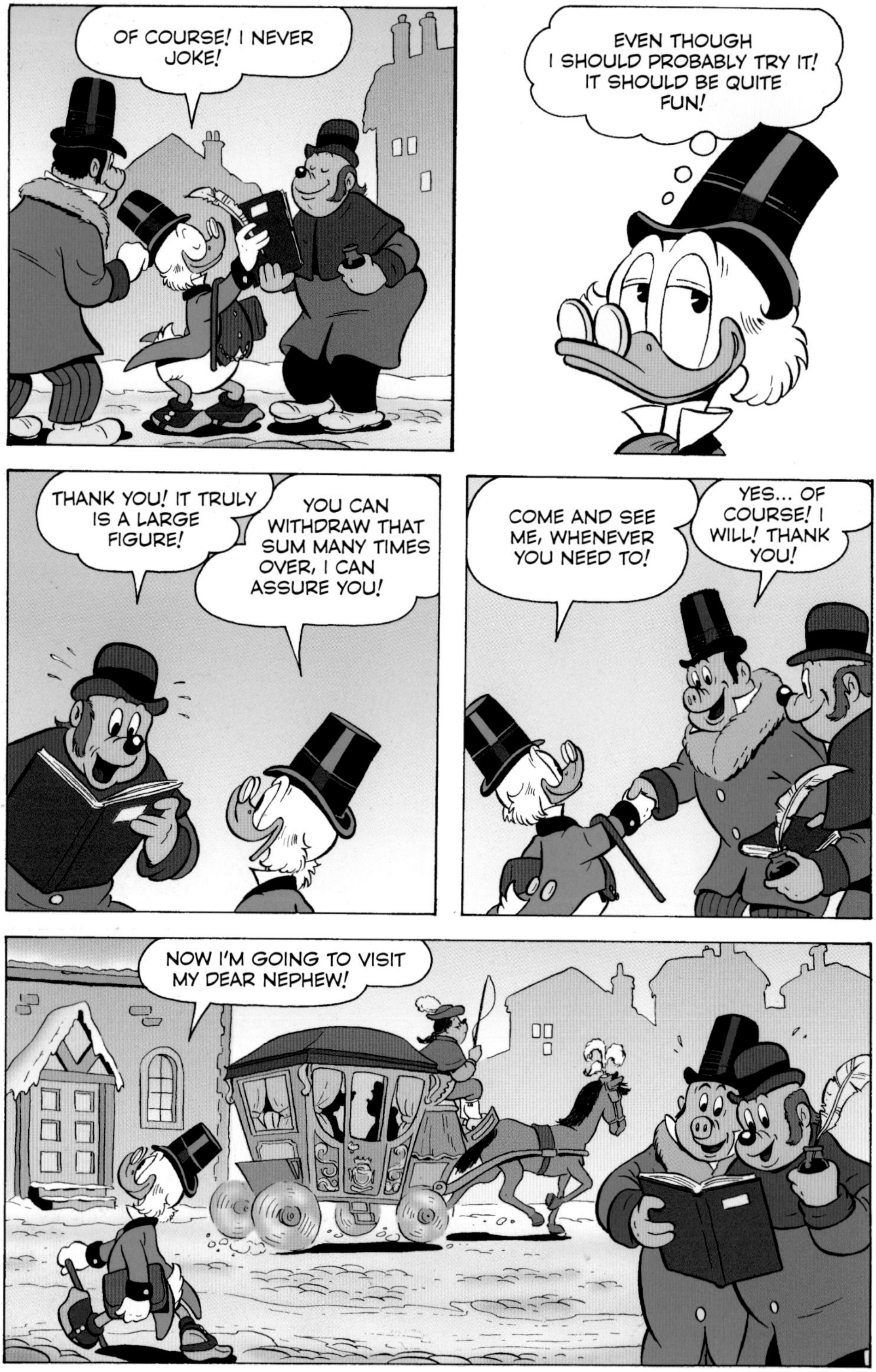
OF COURSE! I NEVER JOKE!
EVEN THOUGH I SHOULD PROBABLY TRY IT! IT SHOULD BE QUITE FUN!
THANK YOU! IT TRULY IS A LARGE FIGURE!
YOU CAN WITHDRAW THAT SUM MANY TIMES OVER, I CAN ASSURE YOU!
COME AND SEE ME, WHENEVER YOU NEED TO!
YES... OF COURSE! I WILL! THANK YOU!
NOW I'M GOING TO VISIT MY DEAR NEPHEW!

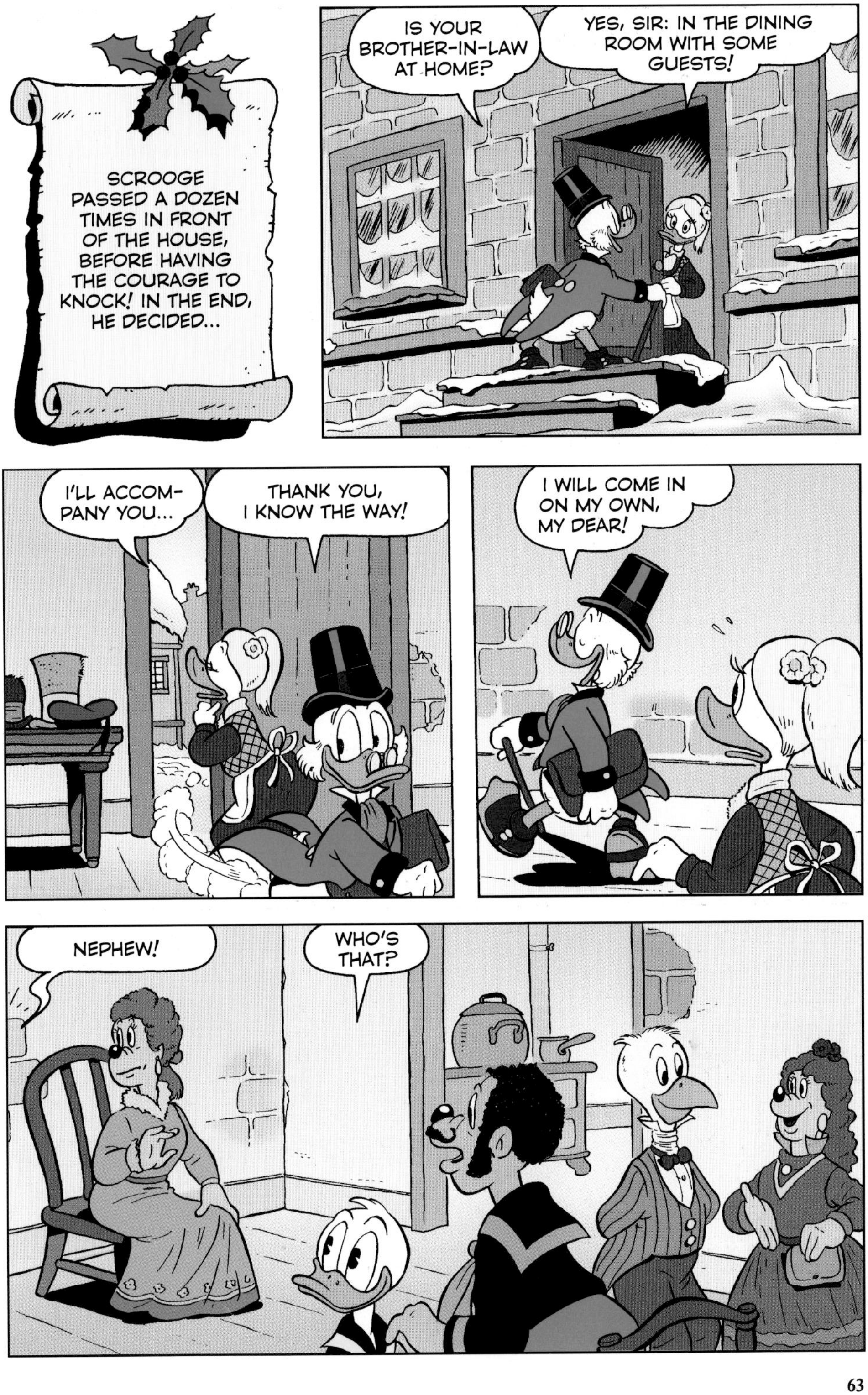
SCROOGE PASSED A DOZEN TIMES IN FRONT OF THE HOUSE, BEFORE HAVING THE COURAGE TO KNOCK! IN THE END, HE DECIDED...
IS YOUR BROTHER-IN-LAW AT HOME?
YES, SIR: IN THE DINING ROOM WITH SOME GUESTS!
I'LL ACCOM-PANY YOU...
THANK YOU, I KNOW THE WAY!
I WILL COME IN ON MY OWN, MY DEAR!
NEPHEW!
WHO'S THAT?

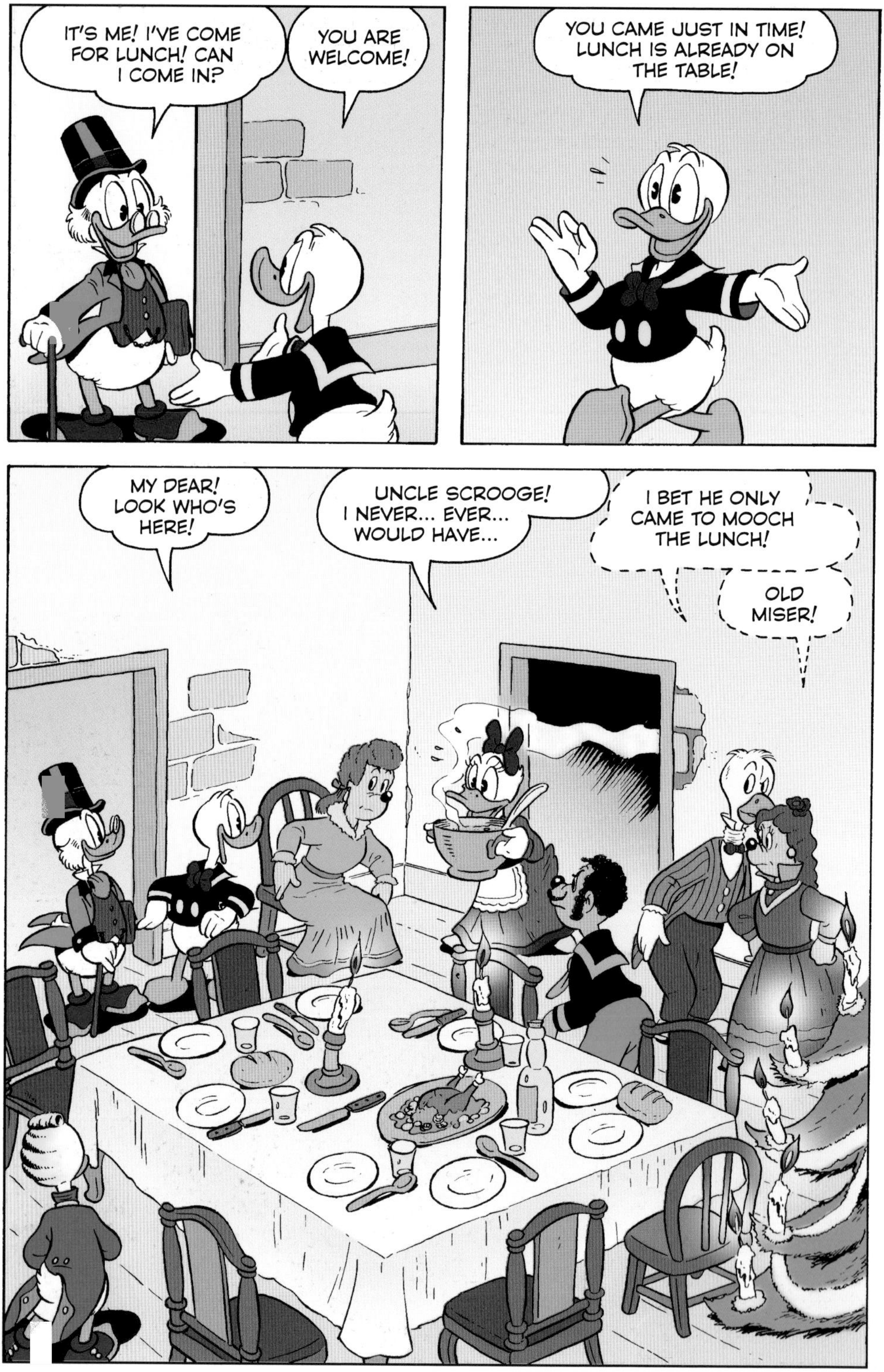
IT'S ME! I'VE COME FOR LUNCH! CAN I COME IN?
YOU ARE WELCOME!
YOU CAME JUST IN TIME! LUNCH IS ALREADY ON THE TABLE!
MY DEAR! LOOK WHO'S HERE!
UNCLE SCROOGE! I NEVER... EVER... WOULD HAVE...
I BET HE ONLY CAME TO MOOCH THE LUNCH!
OLD MISER!

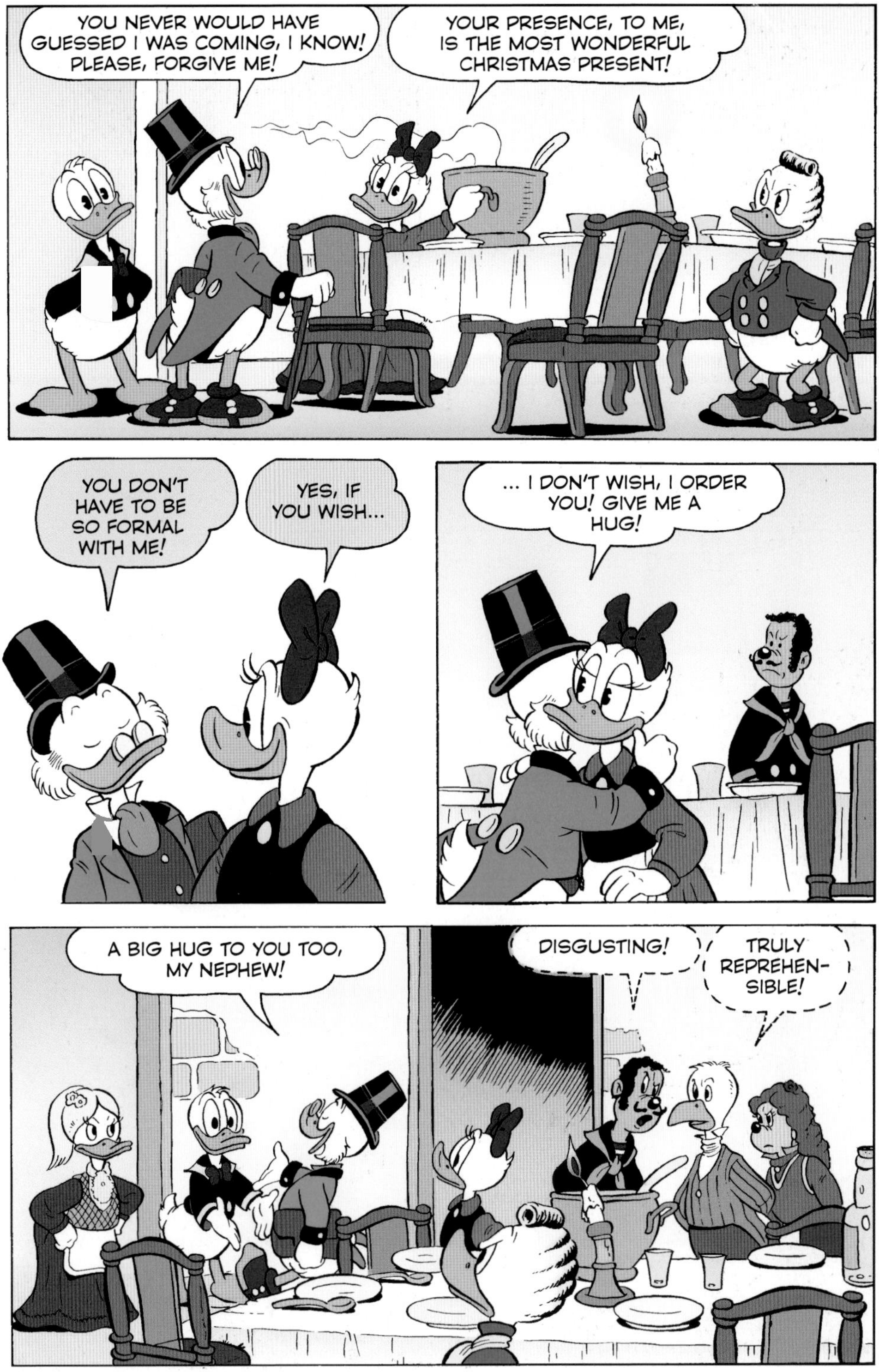
YOU NEVER WOULD HAVE GUESSED I WAS COMING, I KNOW! PLEASE, FORGIVE ME!
YOUR PRESENCE, TO ME, IS THE MOST WONDERFUL CHRISTMAS PRESENT!
YOU DON'T HAVE TO BE SO FORMAL WITH ME!
YES, IF YOU WISH...
... I DON'T WISH, I ORDER YOU! GIVE ME A HUG!
A BIG HUG TO YOU TOO, MY NEPHEW!
DISGUSTING!
TRULY REPREHEN-SIBLE!

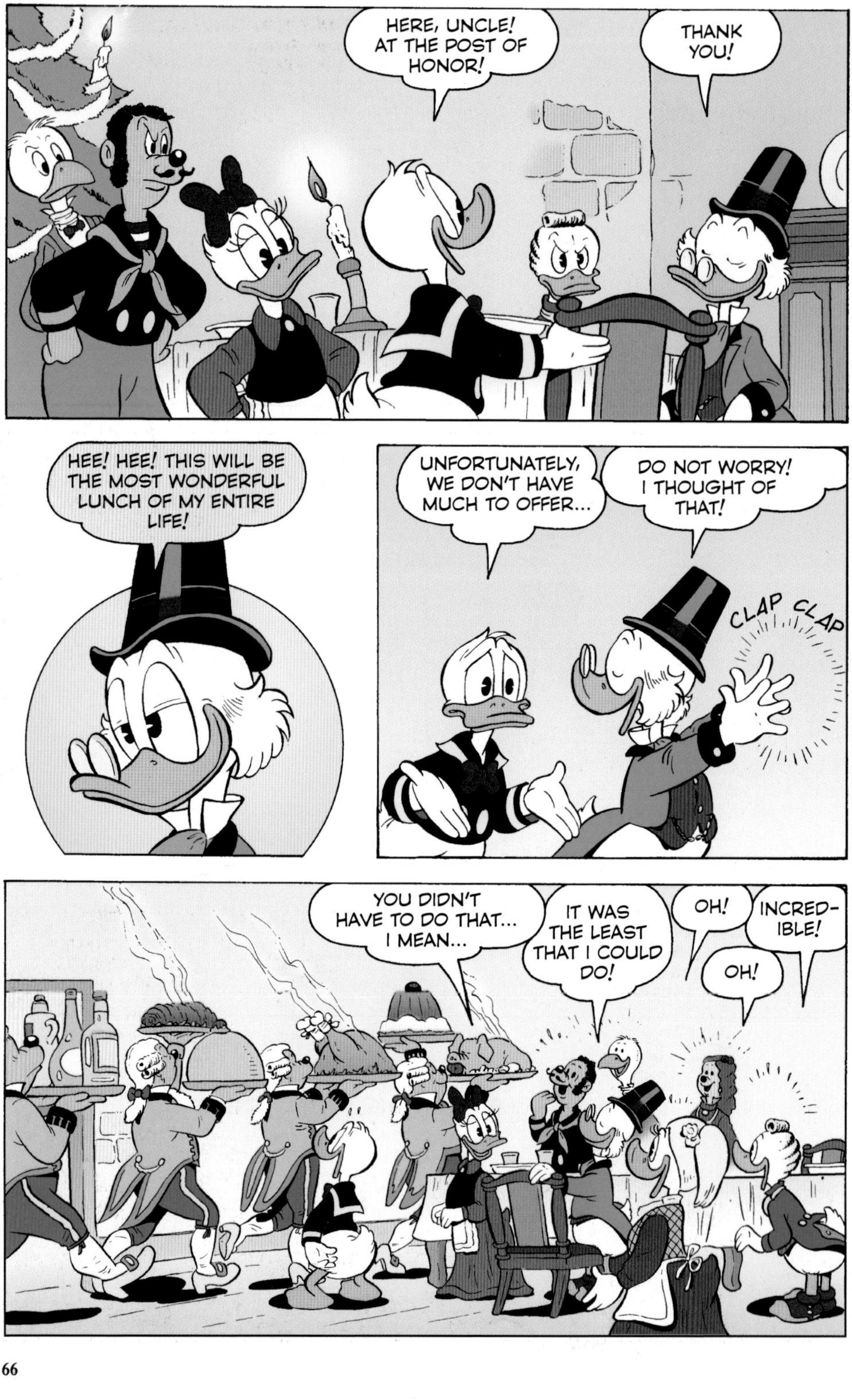
HERE, UNCLE! AT THE POST OF HONOR!
THANK YOU!
HEE! HEE! THIS WILL BE THE MOST WONDERFUL LUNCH OF MY ENTIRE LIFE!
UNFORTUNATELY, WE DON'T HAVE MUCH TO OFFER...
DO NOT WORRY! I THOUGHT OF THAT!
CLAP CLAP
YOU DIDN'T HAVE TO DO THAT... I MEAN...
IT WAS THE LEAST THAT I COULD DO!
OH!
OH!
INCRED-IBLE!

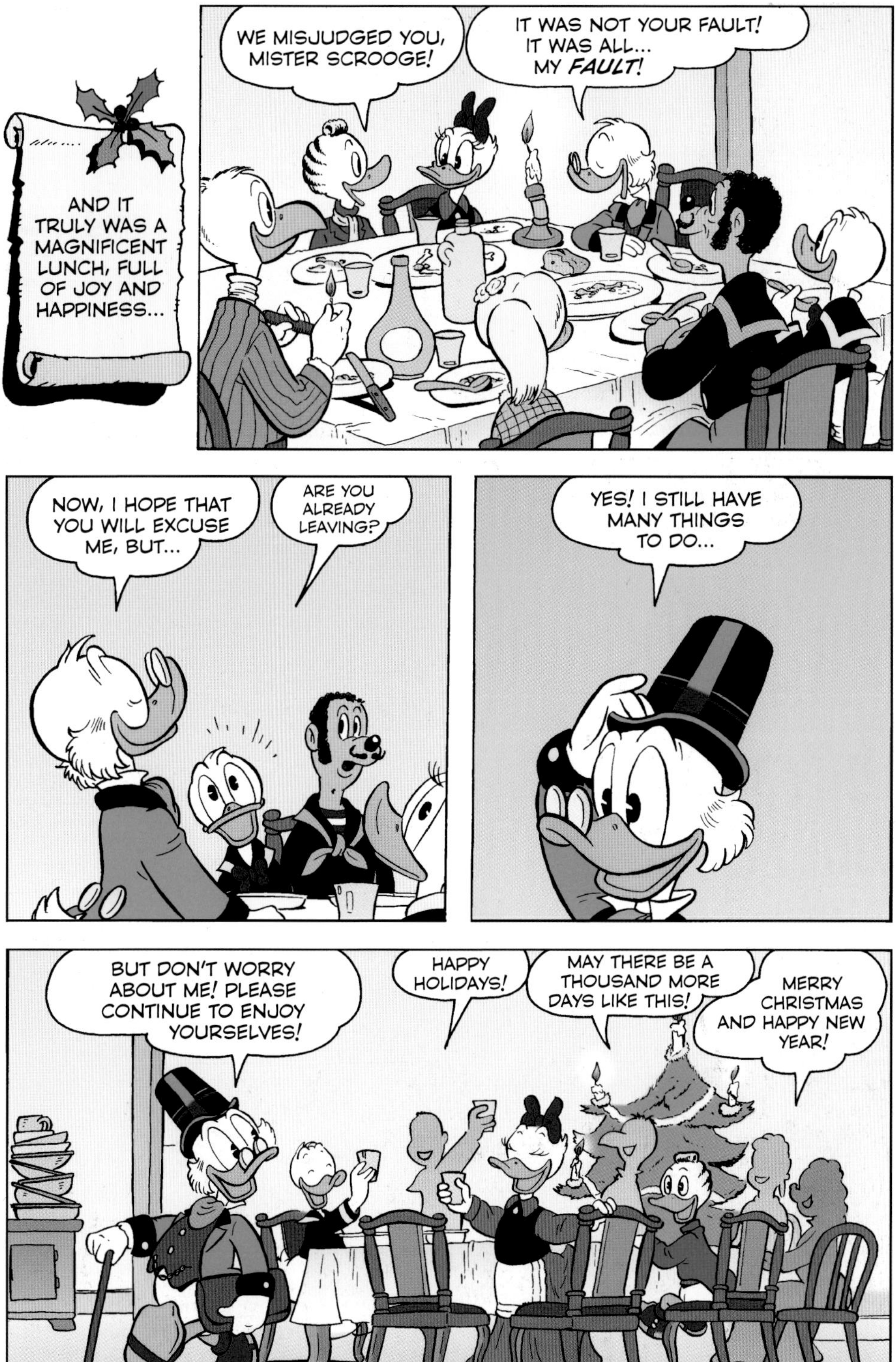
AND IT TRULY WAS A MAGNIFICENT LUNCH, FULL OF JOY AND HAPPINESS...
WE MISJUDGED YOU, MISTER SCROOGE!
IT WAS NOT YOUR FAULT! IT WAS ALL... MY *FAULT*!
NOW, I HOPE THAT YOU WILL EXCUSE ME, BUT...
ARE YOU ALREADY LEAVING?
YES! I STILL HAVE MANY THINGS TO DO...
BUT DON'T WORRY ABOUT ME! PLEASE CONTINUE TO ENJOY YOURSELVES!
HAPPY HOLIDAYS!
MAY THERE BE A THOUSAND MORE DAYS LIKE THIS!
MERRY CHRISTMAS AND HAPPY NEW YEAR!

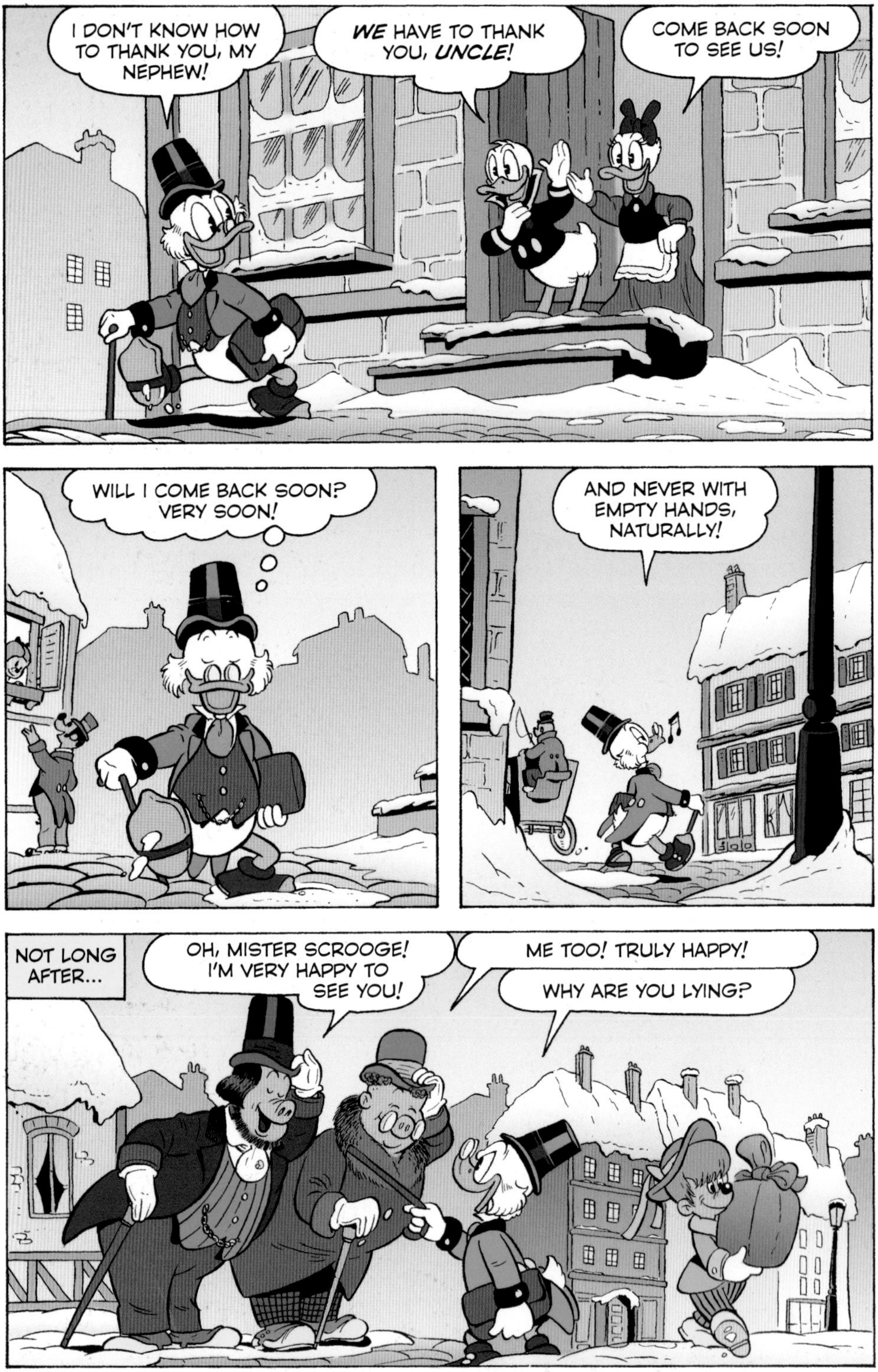
I DON'T KNOW HOW TO THANK YOU, MY NEPHEW!
WE HAVE TO THANK YOU, UNCLE!
COME BACK SOON TO SEE US!
WILL I COME BACK SOON? VERY SOON!
AND NEVER WITH EMPTY HANDS, NATURALLY!
NOT LONG AFTER...
OH, MISTER SCROOGE! I'M VERY HAPPY TO SEE YOU!
ME TOO! TRULY HAPPY!
WHY ARE YOU LYING?

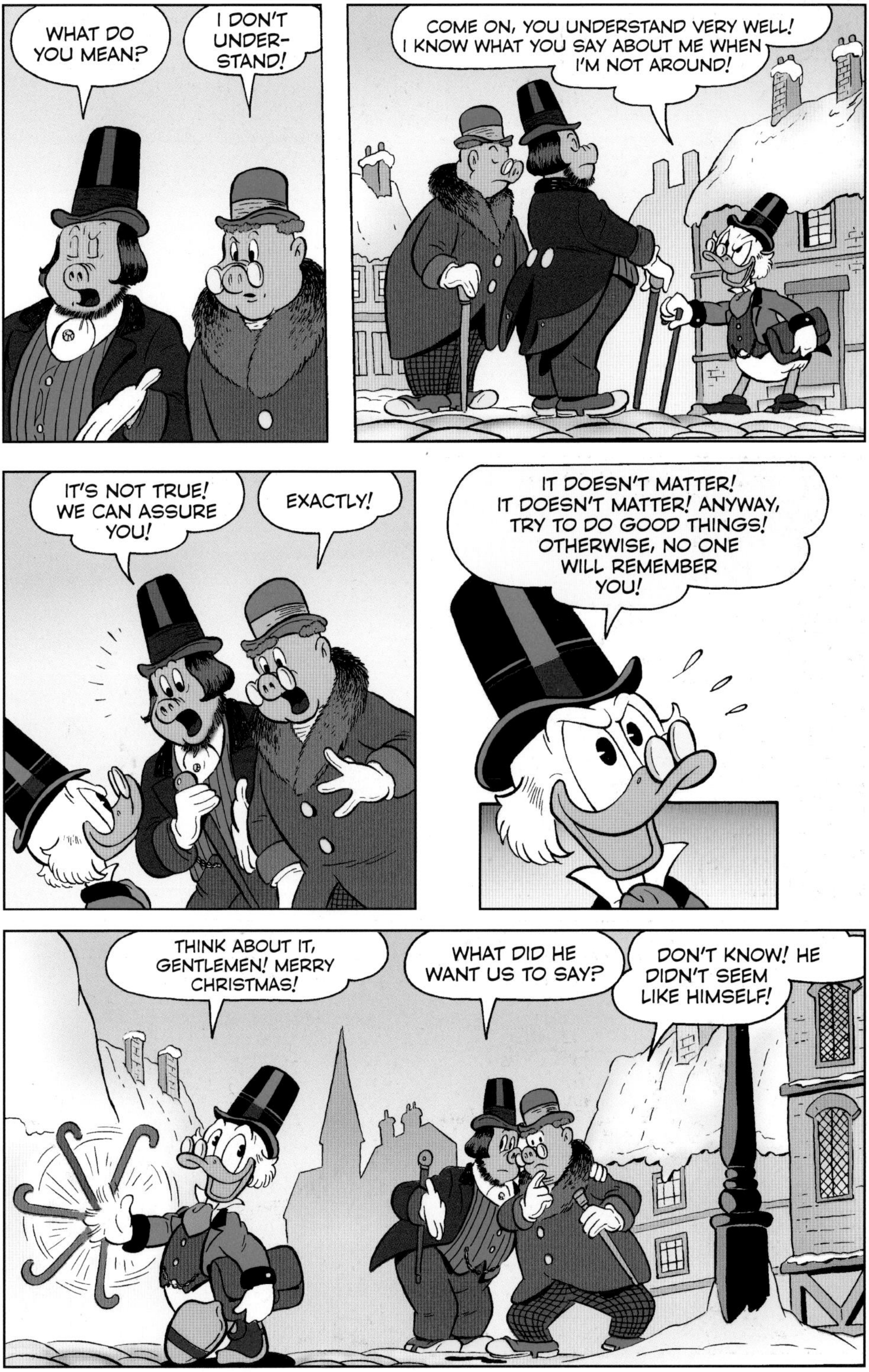
WHAT DO YOU MEAN?
I DON'T UNDER-STAND!
COME ON, YOU UNDERSTAND VERY WELL! I KNOW WHAT YOU SAY ABOUT ME WHEN I'M NOT AROUND!
IT'S NOT TRUE! WE CAN ASSURE YOU!
EXACTLY!
IT DOESN'T MATTER! IT DOESN'T MATTER! ANYWAY, TRY TO DO GOOD THINGS! OTHERWISE, NO ONE WILL REMEMBER YOU!
THINK ABOUT IT, GENTLEMEN! MERRY CHRISTMAS!
WHAT DID HE WANT US TO SAY?
DON'T KNOW! HE DIDN'T SEEM LIKE HIMSELF!

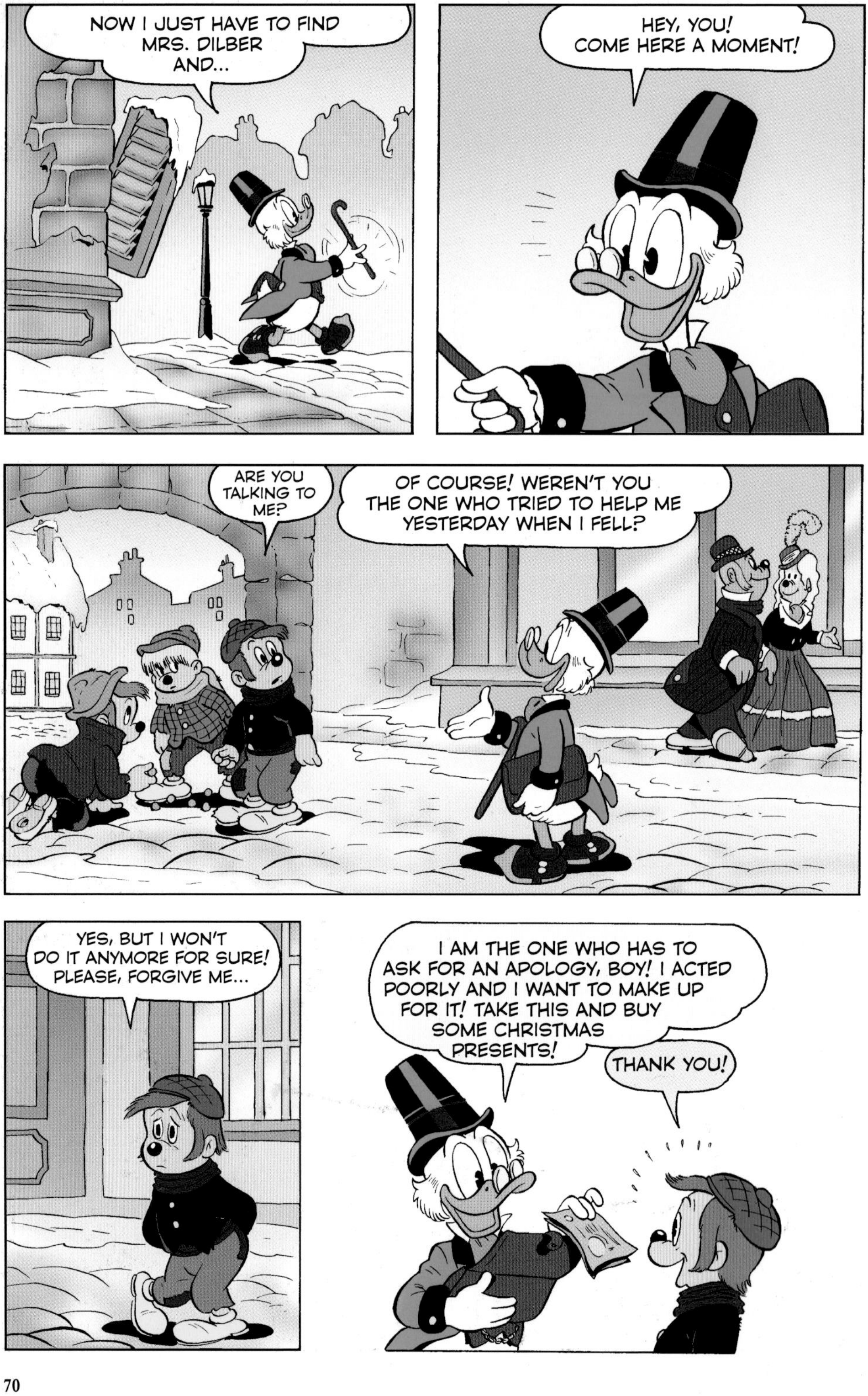
NOW I JUST HAVE TO FIND MRS. DILBER AND...
HEY, YOU! COME HERE A MOMENT!
ARE YOU TALKING TO ME?
OF COURSE! WEREN'T YOU THE ONE WHO TRIED TO HELP ME YESTERDAY WHEN I FELL?
YES, BUT I WON'T DO IT ANYMORE FOR SURE! PLEASE, FORGIVE ME...
I AM THE ONE WHO HAS TO ASK FOR AN APOLOGY, BOY! I ACTED POORLY AND I WANT TO MAKE UP FOR IT! TAKE THIS AND BUY SOME CHRISTMAS PRESENTS!
THANK YOU!

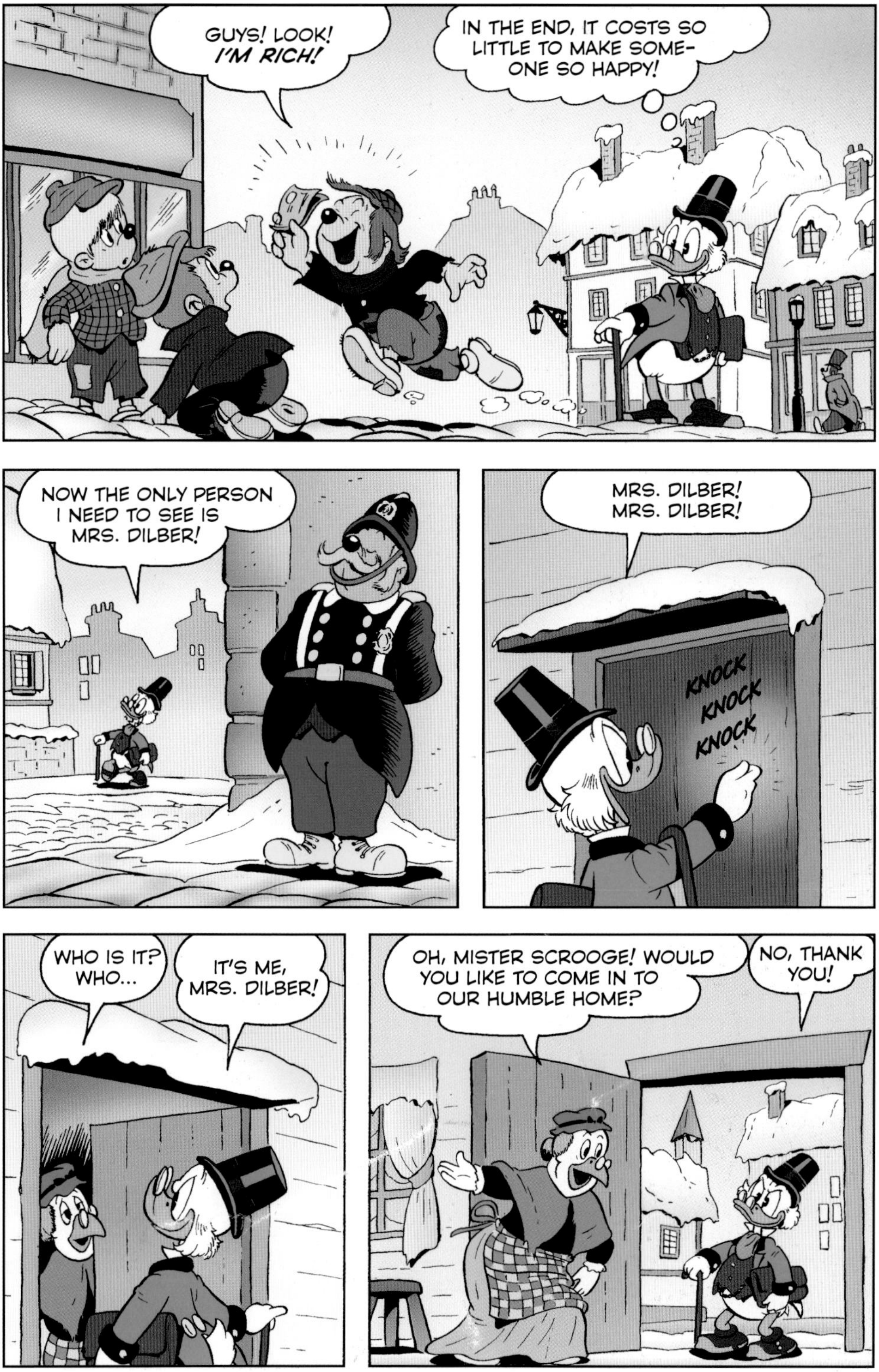
GUYS! LOOK! *I'M RICH!*
IN THE END, IT COSTS SO LITTLE TO MAKE SOME-ONE SO HAPPY!
NOW THE ONLY PERSON I NEED TO SEE IS MRS. DILBER!
MRS. DILBER! MRS. DILBER!
KNOCK KNOCK KNOCK
WHO IS IT? WHO...
IT'S ME, MRS. DILBER!
OH, MISTER SCROOGE! WOULD YOU LIKE TO COME IN TO OUR HUMBLE HOME?
NO, THANK YOU!

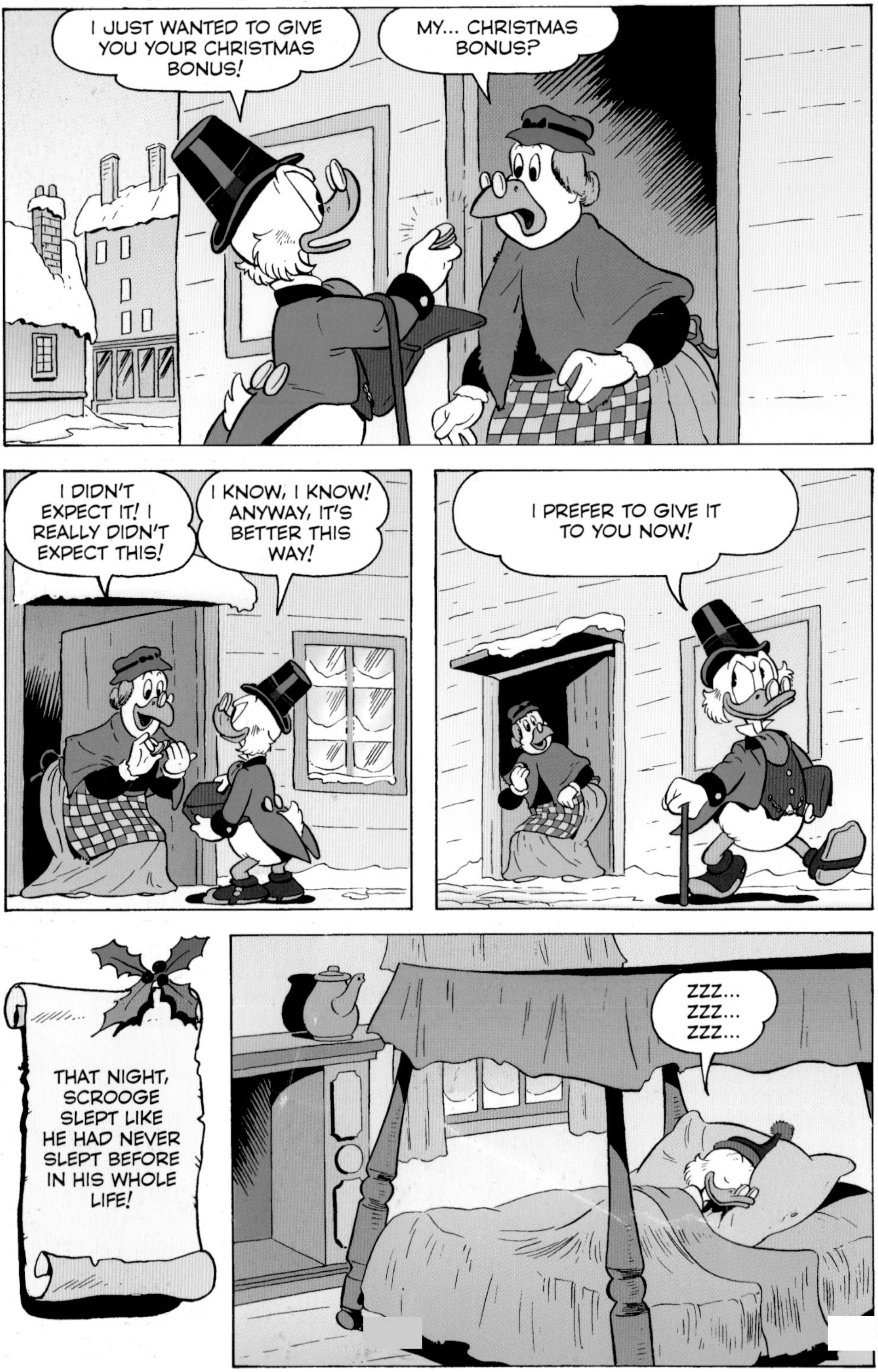
I JUST WANTED TO GIVE YOU YOUR CHRISTMAS BONUS!
MY... CHRISTMAS BONUS?
I DIDN'T EXPECT IT! I REALLY DIDN'T EXPECT THIS!
I KNOW, I KNOW! ANYWAY, IT'S BETTER THIS WAY!
I PREFER TO GIVE IT TO YOU NOW!
THAT NIGHT, SCROOGE SLEPT LIKE HE HAD NEVER SLEPT BEFORE IN HIS WHOLE LIFE!
ZZZ... ZZZ... ZZZ...

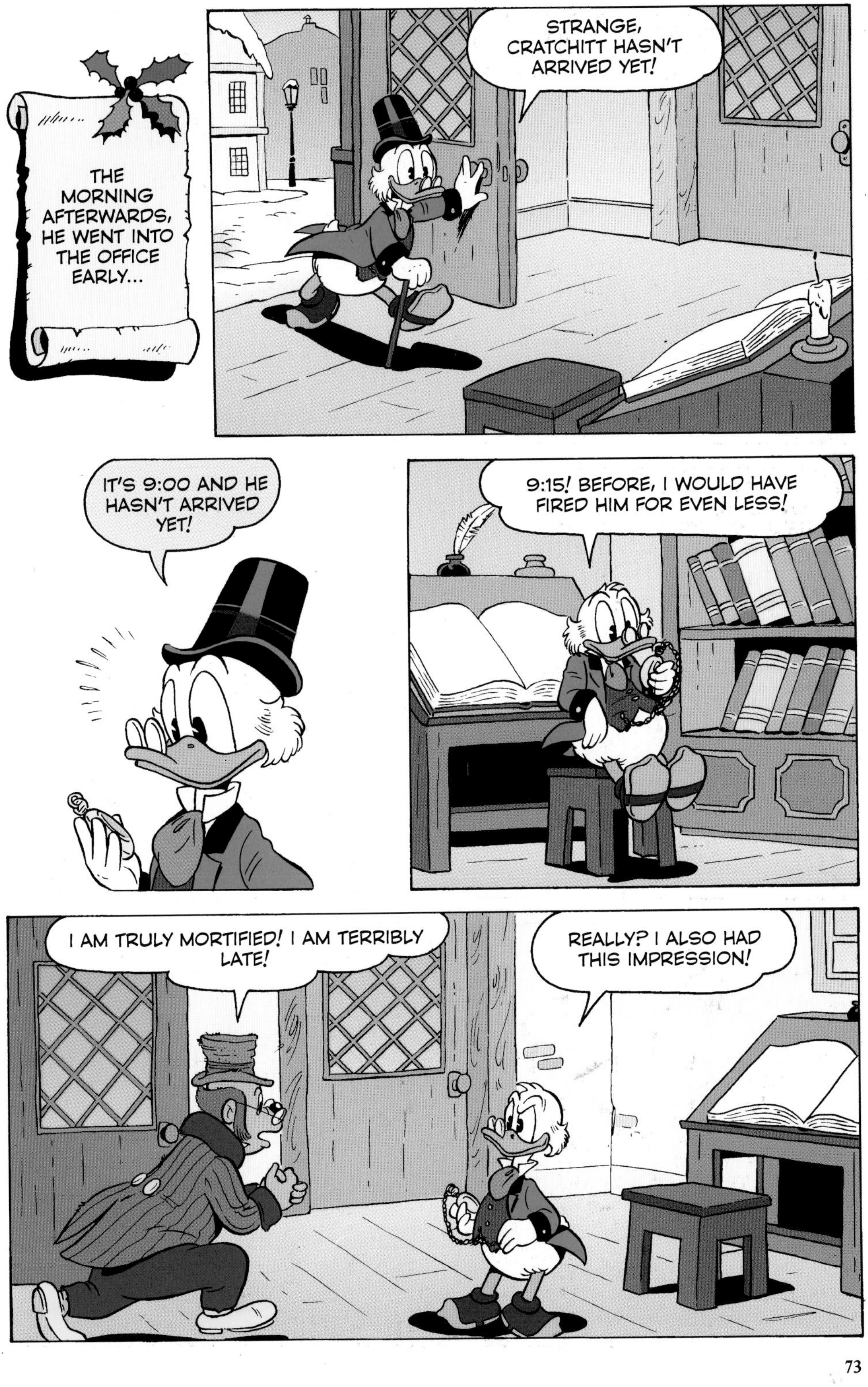
THE MORNING AFTERWARDS, HE WENT INTO THE OFFICE EARLY...
STRANGE, CRATCHITT HASN'T ARRIVED YET!
IT'S 9:00 AND HE HASN'T ARRIVED YET!
9:15! BEFORE, I WOULD HAVE FIRED HIM FOR EVEN LESS!
I AM TRULY MORTIFIED! I AM TERRIBLY LATE!
REALLY? I ALSO HAD THIS IMPRESSION!

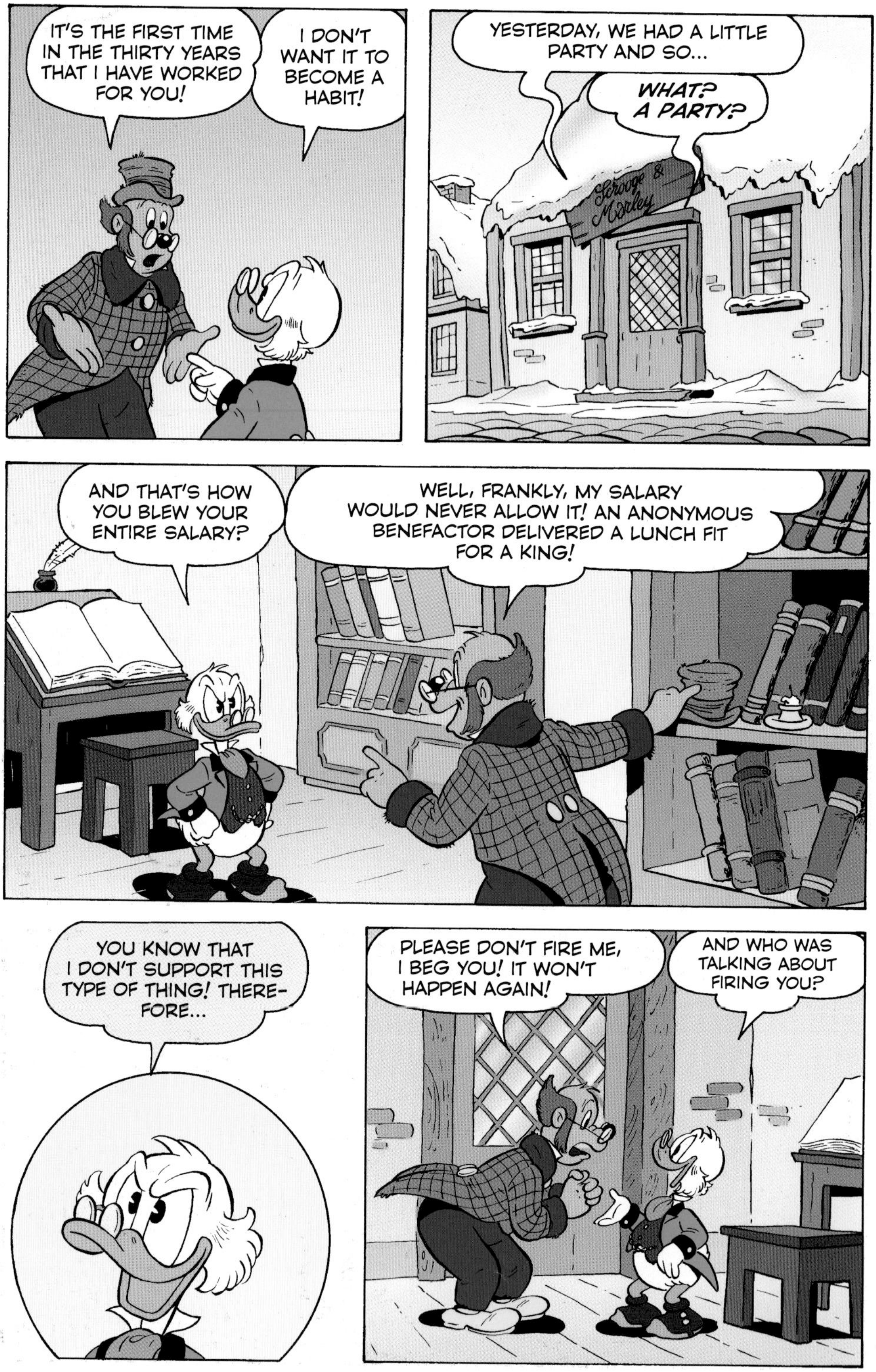
IT'S THE FIRST TIME IN THE THIRTY YEARS THAT I HAVE WORKED FOR YOU!
I DON'T WANT IT TO BECOME A HABIT!
YESTERDAY, WE HAD A LITTLE PARTY AND SO...
WHAT? A PARTY?
Scrooge & Marley
AND THAT'S HOW YOU BLEW YOUR ENTIRE SALARY?
WELL, FRANKLY, MY SALARY WOULD NEVER ALLOW IT! AN ANONYMOUS BENEFACTOR DELIVERED A LUNCH FIT FOR A KING!
YOU KNOW THAT I DON'T SUPPORT THIS TYPE OF THING! THERE-FORE...
PLEASE DON'T FIRE ME, I BEG YOU! IT WON'T HAPPEN AGAIN!
AND WHO WAS TALKING ABOUT FIRING YOU?

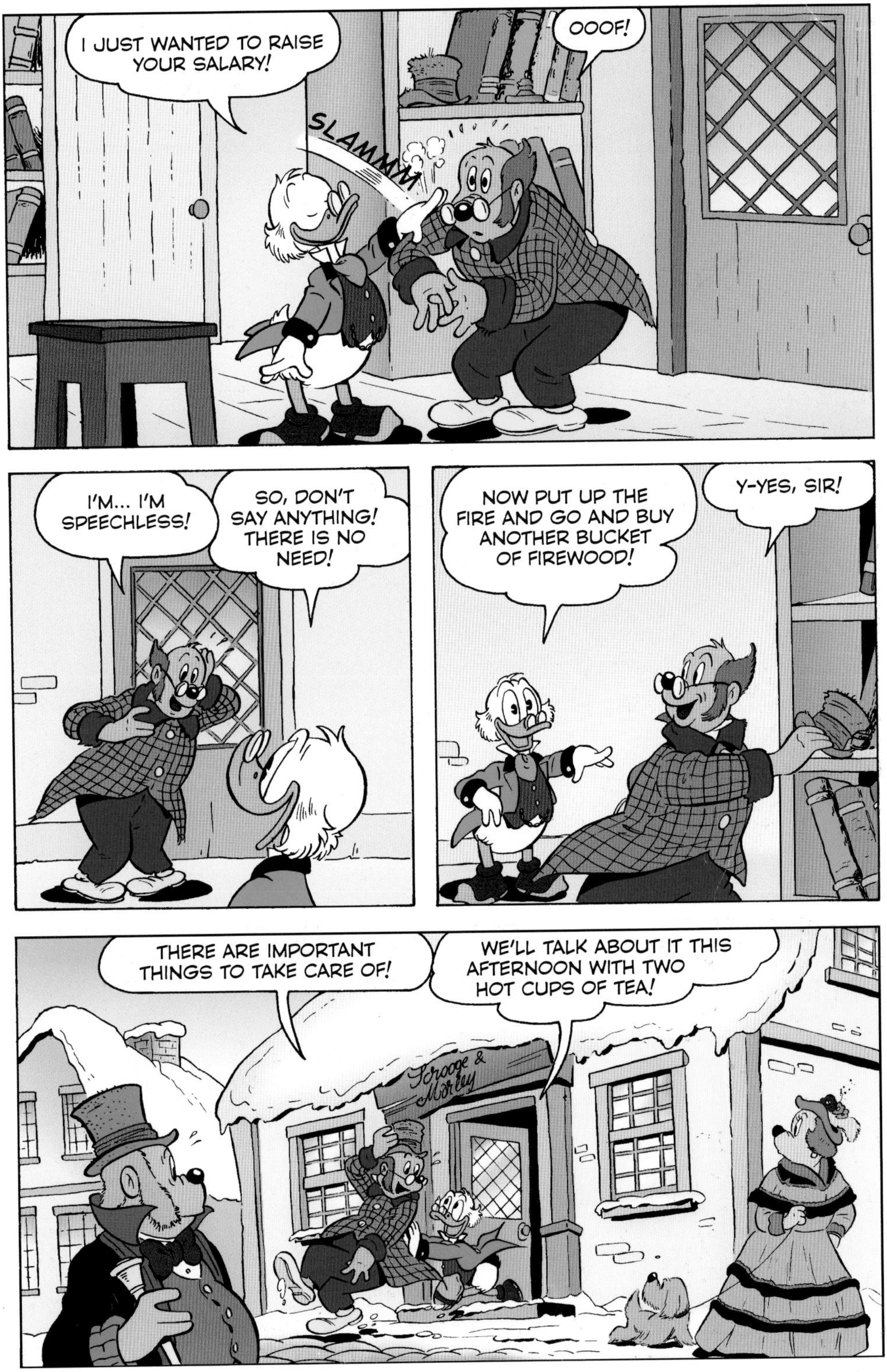
I JUST WANTED TO RAISE YOUR SALARY!
SLAMMM
OOOF!
I'M... I'M SPEECHLESS!
SO, DON'T SAY ANYTHING! THERE IS NO NEED!
NOW PUT UP THE FIRE AND GO AND BUY ANOTHER BUCKET OF FIREWOOD!
Y-YES, SIR!
THERE ARE IMPORTANT THINGS TO TAKE CARE OF!
WE'LL TALK ABOUT IT THIS AFTERNOON WITH TWO HOT CUPS OF TEA!
Scrooge & Marley

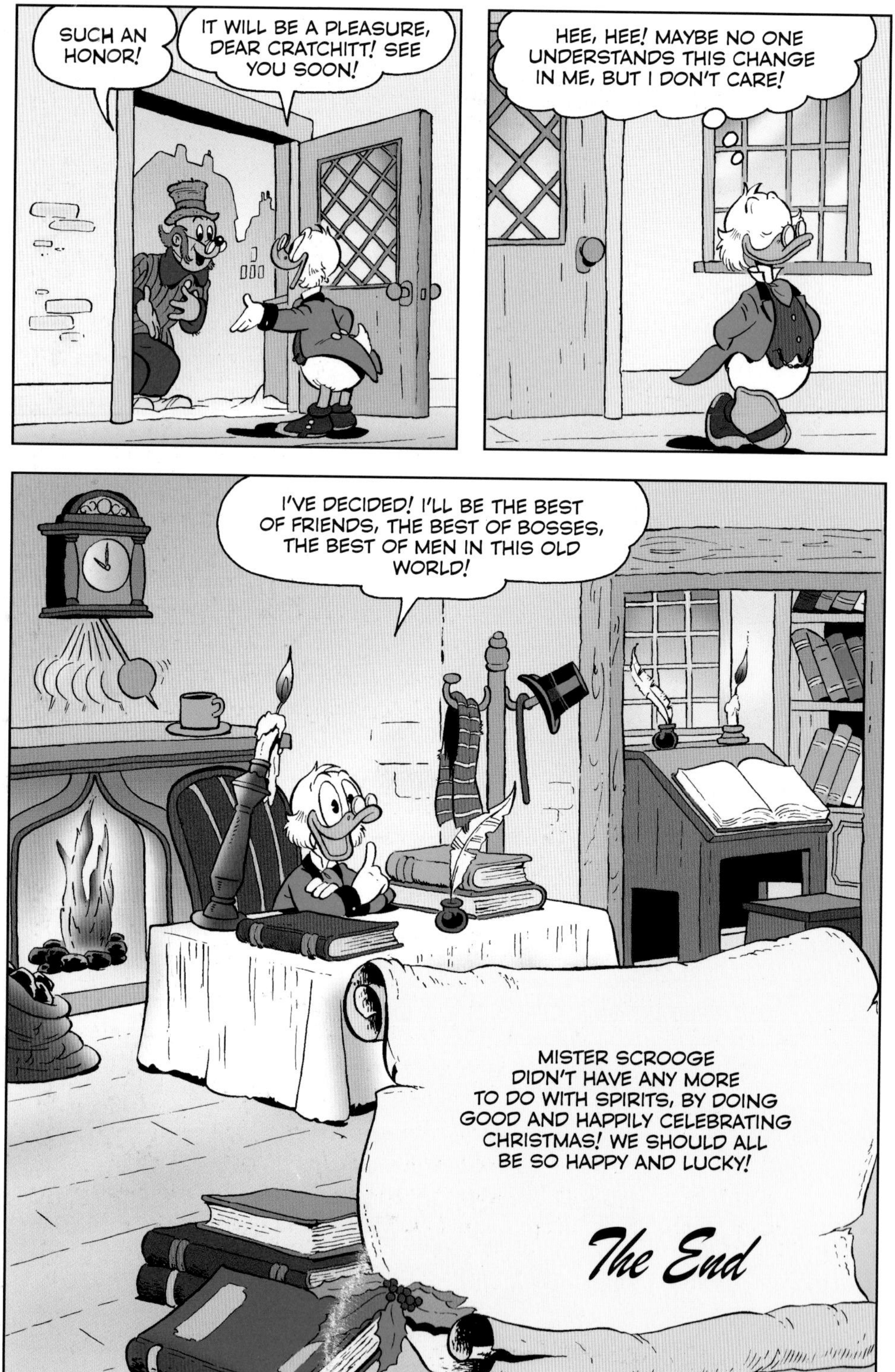
SUCH AN HONOR!
IT WILL BE A PLEASURE, DEAR CRATCHITT! SEE YOU SOON!
HEE, HEE! MAYBE NO ONE UNDERSTANDS THIS CHANGE IN ME, BUT I DON'T CARE!
I'VE DECIDED! I'LL BE THE BEST OF FRIENDS, THE BEST OF BOSSES, THE BEST OF MEN IN THIS OLD WORLD!
MISTER SCROOGE DIDN'T HAVE ANY MORE TO DO WITH SPIRITS, BY DOING GOOD AND HAPPILY CELEBRATING CHRISTMAS! WE SHOULD ALL BE SO HAPPY AND LUCKY!
The End

ABOUT THE ORIGINAL AUTHOR

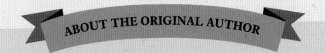

CHARLES DICKENS

(1812–1870)

Charles Dickens was an English novelist in the nineteenth century. A prolific writer, he is best known for his novels *Great Expectations*, *A Tale of Two Cities*, *David Copperfield*, *A Christmas Carol*, and many more.

Born in Portsmouth, England, in 1812, Charles Dickens was the second child in a family of eight children. When he was twelve years old, his father was imprisoned for debts, and Dickens dropped out of school to work at a factory to help support his family. While his family moved closer to the prison, Dickens lived alone and continued to work in poor conditions for three years before returning to school. This experience with hardship and loneliness ultimately became motivation for many of his writings.

Dickens worked as a stenographer, a shorthand reporter, and as a journalist. In 1833, while a reporter with connections to a variety of opportunities to publish his work, Dickens began to contribute short stories and essays to periodicals. For a while he wrote under the pseudonym, Boz; and, in 1836, he published his first book, *Sketches by Boz*.

Also in 1836, Dickens married Catherine Hogarth with whom he had ten children, and he began publishing *The Posthumous Papers of the Pickwick Club*. After the success of *Pickwick*, Dickens's main profession was as a novelist, though he continued working in journalism until the end of this life.

In 1849, Dickens published *David Copperfield*. This novel was his personal favorite and was semi-autobiographical—incorporating elements of Dickens's childhood, career, and love-life.

When Charles Dickens passed away on June 9, 1870, it was a national day of mourning in England. He was one of the most influential voices of his time, known as an advocate for social and economic reform. His novels gave insight to the working class, and explored themes of alienation, social conditioning, and the importance of human values.

Disney

CLASSIC STORIES RETOLD WITH THE MAGIC OF DISNEY!

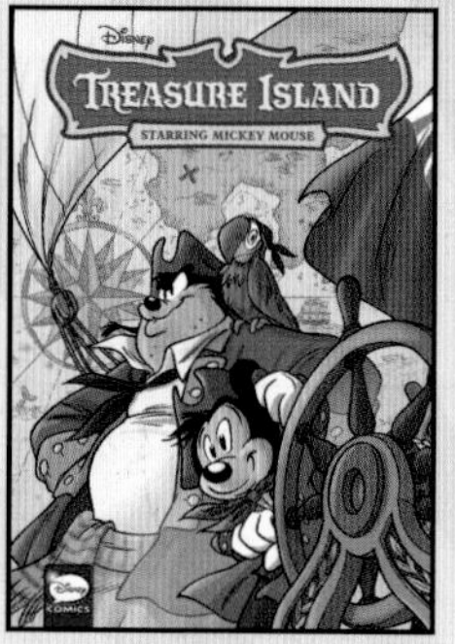
Disney
TREASURE ISLAND
STARRING MICKEY MOUSE

Disney Treasure Island, starring Mickey Mouse

Robert Louis Stevenson's classic tale of pirates, treasure, and swashbuckling adventure comes to life in this adaptation!

978-1-50671-158-4 ✠ $10.99

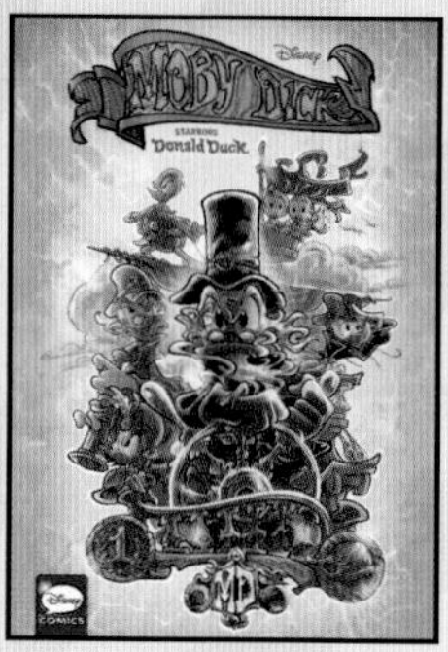
Disney
Moby Dick
STARRING Donald Duck

Disney Moby Dick, starring Donald Duck

In an adaptation of Herman Melville's classic, sailors venture out on the high seas in pursuit of the white whale Moby Dick.

978-1-50671-157-7 ✠ $10.99

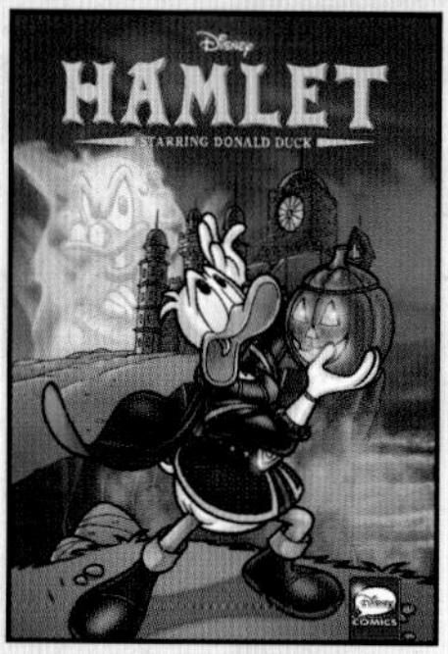
Disney
HAMLET
STARRING DONALD DUCK

Disney Hamlet, starring Donald Duck

The ghost of a betrayed king appoints Prince Ducklet to restore peace to his kingdom in this adaptation William Shakespeare's tragedy.

978-1-50671-219-2 ✠ $10.99

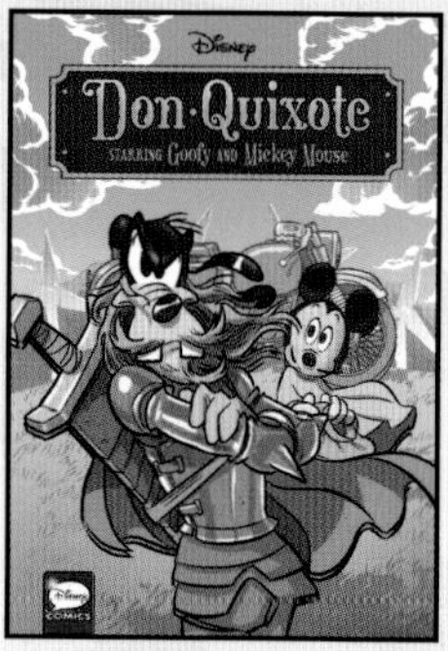
Disney
Don·Quixote
STARRING Goofy AND Mickey Mouse

Disney Don Quixote, starring Goofy & Mickey Mouse

A knight-errant and the power of his imagination finds reality in this adaptation of the classic by Miguel de Cervantes!

978-1-50671-216-1 ✠ $10.99

DARK HORSE BOOKS

AVAILABLE AT YOUR LOCAL COMICS SHOP OR BOOKSTORE! To find a comics shop in your area, visit comicshoplocator.com. For more information or to order direct: ✠ On the web: DarkHorse.com ✠ Email: mailorder@darkhorse.com ✠ Phone: 1-800-862-0052 Mon.–Fri. 9 a.m. to 5 p.m. Pacific Time

Disney COMICS

LOOKING FOR BOOKS FOR YOUNGER READERS?

$7.99 each!

EACH VOLUME INCLUDES A SECTION OF FUN ACTIVITIES!

DISNEY ZOOTOPIA: FRIENDS TO THE RESCUE
ISBN 978-1-50671-054-9

DISNEY ZOOTOPIA: FAMILY NIGHT
ISBN 978-1-50671-053-2

Join young Judy Hopps as she uses wit and bravery to solve mysteries, conundrums, and more! And quick-thinking young Nick Wilde won't be stopped from achieving his goals—where there's a will, there's a way!

DISNEY·PIXAR INCREDIBLES 2: HEROES AT HOME
ISBN 978-1-50670-943-7

Being part of a Super family means helping out at home, too. Can Violet and Dash pick up groceries and secretly stop some bad guys? And can they clean up the house while Jack-Jack is "sleeping"?

DISNEY PRINCESS: JASMINE'S NEW PET
ISBN 978-1-50671-052-5

Jasmine has a new pet tiger, Rajah, but he's not quite ready for palace life. Will she be able to train the young cub before the Sultan finds him another home?

DISNEY PRINCESS: ARIEL AND THE SEA WOLF
ISBN 978-1-50671-203-1

Ariel accidentally drops a bracelet into a cave that supposedly contains a dangerous creature. Her curiosity implores her to enter, and what she finds turns her quest for a bracelet into a quest for truth.

AVAILABLE AT YOUR LOCAL COMICS SHOP OR BOOKSTORE! TO FIND A COMICS SHOP IN YOUR AREA, VISIT COMICSHOPLOCATOR.COM

For more information or to order direct: On the web: DarkHorse.com | Email: mailorder@darkhorse.com
Phone: 1-800-862-0052 Mon.–Fri. 9 a.m. to 5 p.m. Pacific Time

Copyright © 2019 Disney Enterprises, Inc. and Pixar. Dark Horse Books® and the Dark Horse logo are registered trademarks of Dark Horse Comics LLC. All rights reserved. (BL8019)

Looking for Disney *Frozen?*

Disney FROZEN
BREAKING BOUNDARIES

Anna is on a mission to find more ways that she can help the people of Arendelle. When a wild animal disrupts the village, she meets Mari—an adventurous young woman who has similar feelings— and together they decide to explore some of the many different jobs that the kingdom has to offer. Meanwhile, Elsa is occupied with a mystery in Arendelle's western woods and tension brewing in a nearby territory. Anna and Mari, Elsa, Kristoff, Olaf, and Sven, have a quest to fulfill, mysteries to solve, and peace to restore . . . Can they do it?

978-1-50671-051-8 ❄ $10.99

AVAILABLE AT YOUR LOCAL COMICS SHOP OR BOOKSTORE! TO FIND A COMICS SHOP IN YOUR AREA, VISIT COMICSHOPLOCATOR.COM

For more information or to order direct: On the web: DarkHorse.com | Email: mailorder@darkhorse.com
Phone: 1-800-862-0052 Mon.–Fri. 9 a.m. to 5 p.m. Pacific Time

Copyright © 2019 Disney Enterprises, Inc. Dark Horse Books® and the Dark Horse logo are registered trademarks of Dark Horse Comics LLC. All rights reserved. (BL8021)